T0129374

EXILES AT HOME

EXILES AT HOME
JAMAICAN CHRONICLES

The first four stories, plus one

Dereck C. Sale

Trafford Publishing,
Bloomington, IN

www.trafford.com
North America & international
toll-free: 1 888 232 4444 (USA & Canada)
fax: 812 355 4082

This book is dedicated with much love:

to my wife, Birgitta, who traces her love for Jamaica to the evening she landed on the island as a young woman, and lay awake listening to the chorus of a tropical night that no one else heard; and

to our children: Joanna, Juliette, Lisa, and Gregory, of whom we are very proud.

From sweet fields and familiar shores
    I must depart,
Exiled am I from home...
These virgin lands so fairly dressed
Never again shall I...behold
    you even from afar
Yet here, this night, you might repose with me

            Virgil, Eclogues 1.3-4, 75, 80

CONTENTS

LOVE AND LET DIE

1962

Young William Farnam coaxed the fish-monger's truck down the driveway of Stroud Hall Estate. At the bottom, by the iron gates, after much wrestling with gear-stick and steering-wheel, he managed to turn the old Ford around. Full of joy and expectation he retraced his jaunt across the estate's broad frontage dotted with guava. Through the trees, yellow barked in the sun, he caught glimpses of the polo field. Then, once he turned the corner, clearly dominating the top of the hill among royal palms, was the Great House, foundations high in front and low in back because of the hill.

By now, he thought, Emily must be waiting for him. After all, he had instructed Fisher to make sure she was told of his solo outing and imminent return. Without doubt, she would be impressed with his virtuoso performance behind the wheel, if only because he had kept his driving lessons a secret. But, when he brought the truck to a stop amidst a cloud of black smoke in front of the house, Emily was nowhere to be seen. Disappointed, he could do nothing except return the key to his instructor.

Fisher was a short and wiry East Indian, who for many years had supplied fresh seafood to the large estates in the parish. "You drive very good, Mr. William," he said, before seeming to remember something important. "Miss Emily say she will be out, soon."

William felt cheated. His friend's belated consolation could not change that. He must leave quickly, he thought, before Emily appeared.

"What an awful smell!" The shrill voice came from the veranda above them. Descending the front steps was an apparition radiant in a white dress overlaid by shafts of dark curls, tied at the apex and cascading over shoulders.

"Could you not have been here to see me, Emily?"

"Didn't see you, but we heard this man's truck on the hill."

Emily Stroud was always one step ahead of him.

"Well, it's all over now," William said, wanting out. "So come down and thank Fisher for the show you missed."

"Don't get all sulky on me," she said, and, flipping back one of the shafts, revealed a white rose nestling on the side of her head. "Iris was fixing this for me. Like it?"

"Yes, of course," he said, confident the flower was for him. "So are you free now?"

Emily made sure the flower was secure before she answered.

"Sorry, William. Not this afternoon. Actually this is for my ballet class. Daddy and Mr. Thompson are about to drive me."

"Who?"

"Oh, Daddy's Canadian friend - from the air force days."

"Here for the tournament?"

"Yes. He's a publisher. Tells me about the war. So, until next week, then."

"What happens next week?"

She looked at him in mock despair, her head thrust out so close to his that he smelled her perfume.

"My party, dummy. Saturday week, it is. Remember?"

"I forgot," William said, angry with himself for avoiding her blue eyes.

Emily had turned to Fisher who was waiting patiently to be dismissed. "Hello, Mr. Fisher, and goodbye. Thanks for Kingfish, At last."

"You welcome, Miss Emily," the sinewy, diminutive man said, clearly unsure whether he was being praised or scolded.

"But we can't thank you for that smell," the apparition said before it ascended the stairs with a flourish and disappeared into the house.

"If you feel need, take it for another drive, Mr. William," Fisher said with a sigh of resignation.

"Thanks, and don't mind Miss Emily," William said. "Maybe next week - if you come when I'm here."

William saw Fisher off, and, as he turned towards the stables to collect Chestnut, was conscious of someone looking down at him from behind the veranda rail. He waved, and the half-hidden figure waved back. Instinctively, he knew that Miriam Stroud had been there all along and must have overheard all that was said. For it was common knowledge she was never far from her daughter, even if it meant hiding in Emily's shadow.

Not that many people knew this five years ago. William remembered it was her father who had brought Emily to join his class at Holy Rosary Primary. Old man Stroud had died and his son Robert had returned from England with his new wife and young daughter, to preside over Stroud Hall. The soft-spoken gentleman embarrassed William by vigorously shaking his hand in front of a full classroom. *Did you know that our families go back many years? Good to have a fine young chap like you to look after our Emily.* To be sure, his daughter was very charming, even if she was given to pouting when not in control of a situation. *My name is Emily. I'm seven years old* she – she was twirling her pigtails, *and my Daddy was in the Air Force during the big war.*

From their first meeting, William was captivated by this addition to his otherwise dull prep-school class. Delicately appealing, Emily was smart, and fun to be with if he could forget about her age. With birthdays a few months before his, age was one thing she had over him. Another was her worldly ways. She had travelled abroad and lived in a big city he knew only from books.

At first, indifference seemed his only defence - *For me Crown Jewels are girl stuff.* That was not without undesired consequences - *Well, we also rode on underground trains. I suppose you don't want to hear about them either.* But in other ways she could be very kind. Most important, she did not avoid him as some of the other girls did. *If you are a nice boy I'll let you be my soul-mate…* After that, nothing she said or did could discourage him from wanting to be her close friend.

Two years later William's only brother, Martin, left to attend university in Boston, and thereafter Emily's friendship filled the void - three summers all told - until last December. At first he tried to ignore the fact that the friend who left for school in September, came home almost a stranger for the Christmas holidays. Months having passed since then he could no longer deny that her once playful personality was now overlaid with spite.

The sun was fast sinking into the sea beyond the cane fields and the mosquitoes were in full flight when William dismounted Chestnut in order to unlock the wooden gate at Rockwell. The matter was settled. He would not visit with Emily before her party. This decision, he told himself, was final. At the most, he might give into a driving lesson at Stroud Hall. Nothing more.

The back-porch of Rockwell house was filled with the sharp

smell of smoke-rings when he entered via the stairs at the rear of the house. As much as he wanted to, he could not avoid his parents. Norman Farnam was seated in his favourite chair beside the divan on which his wife lay, knitting. A portly man of fifty, he had earned from her the title of "less a plantation owner and more a lord of the manor" because of his preference for rather formal attire. It was not unlike him to be seen riding the plantation on the hottest of days, in jacket and tie. With eye glasses perched low on his nose and pipe on a side-table he must have stopped reading the evening paper on hearing William approaching. But his wife was the first to speak.

"Over at the Strouds, were you, William?"

"Yes, mother."

At forty five Dorothy Farnam was prematurely grey, and quite frail having weathered successive illnesses over the years. But a disciplinarian she had been for as long as William chose to remember. Seeing he had promised to be home by 6:30 and it was now dark, her frown told him she was not about to let him get by unscathed.

Norman Farnam was equally direct as he began packing his pipe. "Is it not too late to be dropping in on them, lad?"

"Emily and I were speaking to Fisher," William said, and almost got to the door before his mother stopped him.

"Sit down, son," Dorothy Farnam said. "We have said it before. Fisher is well meaning but he drinks too much. They all do. In any case, it is not necessary, I repeat not necessary, for you to pal around with him."

"I'm not palling around with him, mother."

William fell into the glider next to his interrogators.

Norman Farnam was tampering loose ends of tobacco. "You know what your mother means."

"Yes, father. That was before I was born."

"No matter, William," Dorothy Farnam said. Then, as an afterthought: "A week on Saturday is the girl's birthday party, is it not?"

"How did you know that?"

Dorothy Farnam hesitated before her admission. "Invitation. Came for you, today."

"You opened it, without telling me?"

"I'm your mother, aren't I?"

"So, father saw it too?"

"I left it to your mother," Norman Farnam said between quick puffs in order to recover from a false light.

"I want it."

"Too much mooning around over there, son."

"So what is wrong with having a good friend, father?"

"Don't get carried away at your age, William."

"I want Emily's invitation before I go to bed, mother."

Norman Farnam had settled down to enjoy his paper and a smoke, but William knew he had not been dismissed.

"You're in high school now, William. Soon you'll be in university. Your brother, Marty, was not much older than you when he left us to study Business and Law. What are you thinking about, besides girls?"

William resented being scolded about schoolwork when everyone knew that study-grades were important to him. So what if they were not as important as they had been for Martin?

"We are good youngsters, father. I just want to be with her."

Dorothy Farnam was busy gathering up her knitting and placed it in a wicker-basket by her side. "Don't get over your head in such friendships, William. Emily lives in a different world from you. For you, cane and cattle are your birthright. Not for her. Understand, son?"

"Seems that avoiding Emily is like avoiding Fisher."

"Don't get smart with your mother, William. Again, you know what she means."

"Too many adult goings-on at the moment, William," Dorothy Farnam said.

"It's not fair. I must give up Emily just because the Strouds are rich? Or just because they party a lot and don't go to church?"

"All airs and graces, that Miriam."

"Just because she runs the estate, mother?"

Norman Farnam had resumed reading the newspaper, only to break off and wag his finger at William. "I bet your Emily wants to wear the pants too."

William disliked the truth, but could not deny it. "Maybe. At the same time, you like the Strouds, father. Mother does too. You're both going to the tournament, aren't you?"

Dorothy Stroud sat up on the divan. "Enough bad-mouthing of our neighbours," she said, looking down and uncovering her legs. "Young people should realize that their future lives will not turn out the way they imagine."

"Yes, Mother."

"Leave your father to enjoy his smoke. Help me up please."

"By the way," Norman Farnam said, addressing the Gazette, "fewer of those "just-because" comments, young man. In the end, nothing important is that simple."

Yet for William, what had happened earlier over at the Strouds was very important. And it had been that simple. He witnessed an angel descend the front stairs of the Stroud Hall Great House and something had registered with him, even if he could not give it a name. Her big party was in twelve days. How could he survive the wait?

"I take it that tomorrow you will be away with Ralph?"

"Yes, mother. To Hopeview in the morning. Glad you don't mind if I go with Ralph."

"He is one of our household staff, William. Do you know that Anvil hurt him today?"

"No. Is he alright?"

"Back-trouble. His daughter, Rajani, is sick too, he says."

"Is she back here? I will see him tomorrow," William said. For now his mind was fixed on the fleeting caress of Emily's face against his. The moment was becoming an eternity of blissful helplessness that bordered on misery.

"Bring my chair, son. And stop mooning," his mother said. "Dinner will be ready soon. Afterwards: to bed with you."

William hoped the trip tomorrow would help him put thoughts of Emily behind him. Ralph had been his confidant since first he accompanied William into the bush to hunt birds. A check on the condition of the northern fences was overdue. This was also Ralph's month to inspect those of Hopeview Estate, the adjoining cattle property owned by a family in Edinburgh.

Next morning William was so tired, it took the high-pitched calls of cattle being driven into the holding-pens to wake him from a troubled sleep, and then the screeching of guinea-hens chasing each other in the yard below his bedroom window to get him out of bed. Still groggy, he washed and dressed, then gave in to the excitement of unpacking his new high powered pellet-gun. Having test-fired and cleaned it until it shone, he made sure there was a box of slugs in his haversack, before trundling down to the kitchen to collect the sandwiches made the previous night for the expedition.

The walkway to the outbuildings passed by the stables. After apologizing to his faithful American Shetland for standing him up, he proceeded to Ralph's quarters beside the bull-yard. There, expecting conquests to be brought to him, Anvil was stomping about, angry that a short distance away another pen full of heifers was beyond his reach. The giant Black Angus seemed unaware that their job was confined to making waste-manure in shifts for the cane fields.

"Anvil is lonely, Ralph," William shouted, as he extracted a steaming mug of bush-tea from the coal-stove outside Ralph's room and deposited it in his doorway. Inside, the old man was sitting on his cot, Bible open on his lap.

"They soon bring a friend for Anvil. Lots of friends for him out there now," Ralph said.

"But not you?"

"Knock me down fi true. Anvil no like anybody except him own kind. Anyhow, me no business round him. Unpredicable he is..."

Ralph rose to collect the tea before retreating to wash his face in a wash-basin by his cot. A man of indeterminate age, he looked much younger than his sixty five years because of his muscular upper-body, close-cropped hair, and a dark, angular face not given to lines. But after two decades as head-man on Rockwell he had suffered a heart attack that forced him to retire and accept household duties.

"I heard about your accident. Are you sure you can walk instead of ride this morning?"

Having deposited the empty mug in the wash-basin, Ralph sat on the cot to put on his boots.

"No horse-riding for me today. Pain me back it would."

"You carry the haversack, then. I've got my rifle."

The fire out, they were still in the yard when two youngsters, leading a cow heavy in calf, approached and prised open the side gate of the bull pen. The reluctant animal was inside, before Anvil - pounding on the mud floor as he snorted at the heifers across the compound - was aware of his new companion.

A blinding morning sun, in a cloudless sky, welcomed them as they set out east along a dirt road dividing cane fields. The air was fresh, even allowing for the strong smell of manure emanating from the fifteen-acre plots of newly planted cane-shoots. William was surprised at Ralph's vigorous stride, given his condition. Beyond the cane, they turned left on to a well-trodden track through cow pastures, where indolent Hereford and Indian cattle grazed - ignoring the white birds that sat on their backs. It wasn't long before Ralph was out of breath and they had to stop.

"After we check Hopeview, allow me visit Matty," Ralph said.

"Yes, of course. Is she sick?"

"No. Rajani with her."

"She's come back?"

"Only visit with her mother. Baby miscarry."

"I see," William said, confident he knew about such matters.

They resumed their north-east trek towards the seaward boundary between Rockwell and Hopeview. Ralph appeared stronger after his short rest. Once they reached the fence separating the two properties they turned south to inspect the condition of the barbed-wire.

"They no care for the animals," Ralph said, pointing to the poor state of the grass on Hopeview beyond the fence.

Although the sun was warm, the air off the mountains was cool, bringing with it clouds that swept across the pastures, converting sunlight into shadows before disappearing. Partly covered in mist the mountainous region of Cockpit Country, with its hundreds of impenetrable hillocks, dominated the far distance. William could think only about Emily, that is, until they drew closer to the woodlands that capped the southern boundary of the properties. Then he thought only of birds.

As always, the plan was to access Hopeview itself through the back-gate up ahead, but even before they reached it they were surprised by the unusual activity beyond the fence. Fresh vehicle tracks in the grass led to a sizeable enclosure cut out of the field and bounded by bamboo poles. Into this area several youths were driving twenty or more horned steers accompanied by a large humped-back bull. At the far end of the enclosure, several women were stacking firewood in and among four cement blocks, while two men nailed cross-beams to poles driven into the ground. In their turn, other youths stood by with metal sheets on their heads.

"Zinc roof," Ralph said.

"What are they building?"

"Look like slaughterhouse."

As Ralph opened the gate in the fence, William's imagination raced ahead of the events unfolding before him. What did the slaughter of a cow involve? At Rockwell, animals were taken away, and no one asked about the process. He had shot birds since he was eight years old. Many of the injured critters he had done-in without thought or regret. But to kill a large animal was a different matter.

"Is that allowed?"

"No one to stop them. Does what Busha order them to do."

Busha was Hopeview's manager. A white man, he was well-known in the district but not spoken of with much affection by those who knew him. William had seen him helping with the horses over at Stroud Hall. Right now there was something else on his mind. Later on, Ralph and he would return through this very field, making it impossible to miss the action if they were on time. He was careful to say nothing about it for fear his curiosity might mean another route home.

Leaving the enclosure behind they again turned north-east, this time towards the furthest seaward extremity of Hopeview, plodding through open pastures, avoiding cattle dung inhabited by horned black beetles.

At length, they came to the boundary, and proceeded south, down the footpath from the corner, checking the fence as they went. They stopped for a rest and a drink only when they reached the trees. Once upon a time, both estates shared this forest, Ralph had told him, but that was before Rockwell cleared its section for cane cultivation.

Then it was up the hill towards Henly. The track was steep, and William noticed that his companion was tiring.

"If you want to stop again..."

Ralph paid no attention. "Henly very important. Soon we 'ave lunch."

At several points, the high grasses and intruding bushes inveighed against their progress, which was further hampered in places where wooden planks supplementing the footpath had been dislodged by water run-off. Below, the fields from which they had ascended were bathed in sunlight. The further they ventured up the hill the wetter it became, and the more pervasive the tall cedars, especially in stretches where they competed for the light. Of game birds, apart from a few fly-overs, they saw none. By the time they reached Hopeview's southern fence and the dirt road beyond, William had not once raised his gun, not even under his favorite canopy.

Thirty minutes east of the Hopeview boundary they were in the village of Henly, which consisted of a general store and bakery. Further on, branching off of the main drag was a narrow path that led to a small clearing with half a dozen shacks. William recognized the area because of the hill, stripped of vegetation in back of it where even now several women scavenged for tree roots. He had been over this ground once before when he accompanied Ralph on a visit to his estranged wife.

"Matty place is that one - if you remember," Ralph said, out of breath as he pointed to the yard at the back of the clearing where a zinc-roofed structure with a half-finished veranda stood out among the other dwellings. "We can lunch there."

William was more concerned about the exhaustion evident in

his companion's face. "Equally important, you will be able to rest."

In front of the dwelling two boys sat, one behind the other, rowing a straw-basket. Off to the right, a group of girls played hopscotch. From a vantage point beneath the veranda a mangy black dog barked at the intruders in short bursts, careful to show itself only momentarily. As they entered the yard, the playing stopped. One of the rowers, quite naked, disembarked and approached them.

"Want me call 'er?"

Patting the child on the head, Ralph was about to knock at the front door, when a sprite grey-haired Coolie woman opened it. William knew Matty from her visits to Rockwell. She looked tired and drawn, and the hairs over her mouth were more visible than when he last saw her.

"How she doin, woman?" Ralph asked.

"Thanks for coming. Raj, she very tired," Matty said. "I will ready her in few minutes," she continued, ushering them into the dwelling before she spoke to Ralph. "She want private, so I will tell 'er about him."

The room they entered was small, with a threadbare couch, and a table with two chairs. William had not seen Rajani since he was ten years old. He remembered the day she came to tell Ralph she was leaving the district to find work in Kingston. She had worked on and off as a domestic on the estate, and even stayed with him on one occasion when his parents were at a function in town.

He knew that they would not approve of this visit, certainly not to see Rajani in bed. Uncomfortable, he busied himself by hiding the rifle behind the couch and helping Ralph unload his haversack. Hushed exchanges could be heard beyond the door to Rajani's room, before her mother appeared and ushered them in.

The room was dark and smelled of disinfectant. Matty was quick to fold down the top half of the cloth covering the only window, letting in enough light to reveal Rajani on a cot, propped up by pillows. Her head was strategically covered in bandages that allowed her thick hair to spill over the side of the cot. She seemed older, darker, and heavier than William remembered, especially when he noticed she had no front teeth. More disturbing were the bruises on her face and arms, and the bloodstained bundle in the corner.

"Hello, Rajani," William said.

Without looking at him the distraught figure on the bed retreated into the pillow, before mumbling to her mother.

"I tol' you I prefer not see him."

Matty ignored the comment and collected her shoes from beneath the bed. "This is your problem, father. I going now." After she had departed, Ralph turned to William.

"Please wait next door, Misser William. Sandwich are in the haversack."

Reluctantly, William obeyed, closing the door behind him as he left. Once in the room beside Rajani's, however, he realized how hungry he was, and dove into the haversack even before he was seated at the table. At first he was happy only to eat. Over time, he was distracted by the muffled noises coming from next door, noises that became words he could decipher.

More than once he could not help but hear what was said. Rajani was crying as she spoke, and Ralph was trying to calm her down. William's interest spiked when he heard the name of Busha, punctuated by the sobs.

It soon became clear to him that the person responsible for her condition was the manager of Hopeview Estate. Why Busha would take advantage of a former servant woman was a mystery; but, given his reputation as a bully, apparently nothing was beyond him. The question still remained: What had happened?

Thirty minutes passed before Ralph emerged from his daughter's room. Tight mouthed and red eyed, he reached for the haversack and pointed to the gun behind the sofa. When they left the house he was so grim, and seemed so deep in thought, that William was afraid to speak to him. Ralph ate his lunch in silence as they walked down the track from the settlement, to the dirt road bordering the estates.

"Should kill him," Ralph said finally.

"Better not, Ralph. That's a crime."

"Busha no care about crime."

As they progressed down the boundary-road, William was trying to make sense of what he had seen and heard.

"Why did he beat on Rajani?"

"Man-power over woman. Some want woman as slave."

"Why?"

"No like that God make woman to catch him."

"Catch men?"

"That be woman-power, alone."

"I don't understand."

"To make baby, sar."

"I saw it in the corner, Ralph."

"You hear what Rajani she say?"

William felt Ralph's anger. This was the reason he wished Busha dead. "Not really....I only..."

"Leave it be then, sar. Busha very bad man. Leave it be."

The air was cool, and wet from the mist off the southern hills. William was anxious to see if birds were around, but Ralph seemed reluctant to return by way of the Hopeview forest, through which they had come earlier. By the same token, he seemed very preoccupied, saying nothing until William's favourite spot beneath cedars and beech was within sight.

A rush of wings indicated it was too late to turn back. Caught between strides the two of them stood very still as they scanned the mixed greenery above for a sign of life. William prayed his unsteady companion would reach the canopy without being heard. Slowly they advanced until they were under cover. While Ralph scoured the branches above for movement, William focused on a giant cotton tree that stood tall and alone from the other trees, its stubby limbs covered in Old-Man's Beard.

"Maybe flown," Ralph observed in a whisper.

William knew better. He had seen movement. Almost undetectable against the bark of the cotton tree, there it sat: stately, motionless, and apprehensive - a Bald Pate - sitting partly hidden on a branch high above the forest floor. Signalling silence with his left hand, he stopped awkwardly in the middle of a step and waited. A few seconds later, he was excited to see his target clearly for the first time.

Now, more secure than before, the dove was content to strut its grey-blue plumage backwards and forwards on the branch. Slowly, William raised the rifle to his shoulder and held it there with the bird in the sights, waiting for it to stop and turn around. Then he squeezed the trigger until the crack broke the silence. The dove did not move, except to plummet to the ground at the base of the tree.

"Good size this one," Ralph said, stroking the carcass that he found nestled amongst the exposed roots, before he passed it over to William.

Across both his palms, William cradled the still warm, eiderdown remains - dark eyes staring in stark surprise. Then, with the help of newspaper wrapping, he deposited the carcass in the front pocket of the haversack. "Should be lots more of these out there today," he said.

Not so. That morning he managed to make only two more kills - both pea doves, both smaller than the Bald Pate. Unusual for William, three in total were enough. Today there was something besides birds on his mind. As one o'clock approached, he was unable to think of anything except what might be happening in a field below them.

"We must go back, quickly," William said, as an urgency fuelled by a strange feeling of guilt compelled him forward. He was surprised, as well as a little relieved, that Ralph's thoughts seemed to be somewhere else as they emerged from the footpath. That is, until the field with the newly built structure came into view and they heard the thud of hoofs and the shouts of cattlemen.

"We should hurry home, Misser William," Ralph's concern was evident in his tone.

"They are trying to rope one of the heifers," William said.

"Yes. And that is enough for young peoples."

"I must see what happens. Please."

"The Missis would not like it," Ralph said, concern evident in his defensiveness.

"Mother? She only knows what I tell her." William, with an unhappy Ralph tugging at his arm, stopped by the bamboo fence not far from the wooden structure that had been fitted with the zinc roof in their absence. On this return leg of their walk it was on the near side of the pasture. "We can see better from here."

The noise from the enclosure drowned out the old man's response. Several youths, armed with crude whips, were having fun running among the animals, now visibly nervous and instinctively aware of imminent danger. Wild-eyed and fearful, the steers were charging about in every direction in order to get away from tormentors screaming obscenities.

"Time to go now," Ralph shouted above the noise.

Fixated on the action before him, William refused. "Then, you go."

Ralph hesitated, then decided to remain. The full import of his decision to stay began to test William's resolve as he saw Ralph standing there dejected, his jaws clamped shut, his high bony forehead glistening with perspiration. But there seemed to be no exit. An approaching pick-up truck was already inciting shouts from the labourers and barefooted youth standing outside the bamboo fence; shouts that echoed off the side of the nearby hill:

"Them come, them come now."

The surprise was the two horsemen, riding bare-back, who captured the spot-light. Outflanking the vehicle, they hurtled over the bamboo fence and galloping around the enclosure. By the time they tethered their mounts to the side of the wooden structure, the pick-up had disgorged two white occupants, one a short, curly-haired man carrying a slim leather pouch, and the other, a tall, ginger-haired man of middle age, whom William recognized as Busha from the tasselled case on his hip that was supposed to house a Bowie knife. He claimed it had been handed down to him as eldest son, in memory of an ancestor and Confederate soldier who was killed in the American Civil War.

"No expect to see him," Ralph said. "Myself is very angry. Doan want to see him just yet."

William saw that his companion was perspiring as he looked away from where Busha was standing. But everyone had been galvanized into action by the new arrivals. One of the older black women lost no time in lighting a fire in the rock furnace. Once the flames appeared she ordered that four kerosene tins of water in the back of the truck be offloaded and set on the cement blocks over the fire. Last of all came several rolls of plastic sheeting, which the younger women proceeded to nail to the walls of the makeshift structure.

The man with the Bowie Knife stood against the fence with fists clenched at his side, taking no active part in the proceedings except for a short consultation with the two horsemen. The taller of the two seemed content to stroke a curled bull whip that he had taken from the truck, while the other man, carrying a rope over one shoulder, took charge of the pen by ordering the youngsters to leave the area. This other was heavy-set, with thick fore-arms, and a gold tooth visible when he shouted. Without further delay, he began to circle the animals, already nervous from their earlier harassment, his preliminary rope-throws at stragglers making all of them more so.

Busha had chosen the victim. Somehow, that steer, a shiny black one with muscular shoulders and broad buttocks, realized it had become the hunted. Panicking, the animal began boring and scurrying among the shifting herd in a desperate attempt to hide. In the end there was no escaping the rope thrown around its neck.

Having secured his catch, the rope-man was immediately joined at the rope by his accomplice and two onlookers. Together they succeeded in extracting the steer from its fearful companions. One could see that the doomed animal was aware of its fate and not about to cooperate with its executioners. Desperately, it resisted both rope and forward movement, hugging the ground, head down between front legs fully extended for maximum traction, but with raised hindquarters an easy target. Forward movement was tortuously slow, during which multiple strokes of the tall man's bull-whip produced grudging results.

From behind the fence not far from the shed, William viewed the trauma with fascination now blunted by regret that he was a party to this torment in slow-motion. He nudged closer to Ralph while remaining hypnotized by, unable to look away from, the proceedings in the pen. He had wished to see the Devil's work. Now, with their cords of hemp, and blade unsheathed, the Devil and his angels were about to reward him. Twenty yards from its dreaded destination the unfortunate animal had dug in one last time, refusing to move.

Under the whip and snorting from dust and strangulation, the victim strained against the rope that was now wrapped around one of the posts. For an agonizing moment the heifer's forward movement ceased, that is, until the heavy-set man grasped its tail in both hands and broke it. The stricken animal leapt forward in pain allowing the man with the rope to shorten it.

Again and again the procedure was repeated, until the animal was at the entrance to the shed, inside which the man with the leather pouch stood at the ready. With eyes bulging as much from terror as from lack of oxygen, and its muscles drawn like knots on shoulders and hind quarters sapped of all strength, the victim arrived at the inevitable door, its last effort to hold its ground thwarted by one of the bystanders applying a pointed stick.

"Don't damage him too much," the man called from the within the shed.

William felt his stomach heave. "I want to go home." He took hold of Ralph's arm as they retreated across the open-land next to the pen. All he wanted was to be as far away as possible from what was about to happen. But Ralph could not run fast enough for them to escape the mournful wail that filled the air before an eerie silence descended.

"You cannot tell mother or dad about this, you hear, Ralph?"

"No, will not. Trust me."

"I must tell Emily," William said. Suddenly nauseous, he held his stomach and pretended not to see the wry smile that Ralph was trying to suppress as they crossed the property line into Rockwell.

"Best that way."

"I've done a bad thing, Ralph."

"Not to worry, Misser William."

"What will she think of me?"

"Miss Emily understand. She older than yourself."

 Ralph had touched that recurring sore-point.

"Not really. By just a few months!" William said.

"Beyond her years. Almighty God make them so."

"Difficult to understand, sometimes." William was even more dejected now than before.

After some reflection, Ralph was solemn. "I think the Man say: *Who you doan' understand is older than you.*"

That Emily was somehow grown-up and he not, was a suggestion that never failed to cause him pain, and yet, deep down he knew it to be true. Shortly, she would be thirteen, which, if not confirming Ralph's point, underlined a hard fact of life he must endure until his birthday. Unhappy, but not wanting to make this reality dampen the excitement of seeing her next weekend, he was determined to put it behind him.

It was enough that they were through the gate into Rockwell and on the track north beside the fence. Returning home just as tea was being served on the back- porch was a welcome prospect. For the moment the horrific scene he had just witnessed receded from view.

Emily's party was some eleven days away. William was about to renege on his decision not to visit Stroud Hall before the great event, when she telephoned.

"I am hosting a pre-party, Thursday - day after tomorrow. Can you come over and help me?"

William's heart was pounding. He must not sound too eager.

"What's a pre-party?"

"For the children, dummy. We have eight, what with the tournament guests here, plus four local friends."

"And the grown-ups?"

"They will be at a conference. Come at 4:00, in dungarees."

William could hardly believe his good fortune. All it had taken was a telephone call and the lengthy wait to see her was cut short. Thursday arrived at last, and he found himself on the front veranda of the Great House, in charge of a juice-stand. Emily, confident in her favourite red shorts and close-fitting top, was determined to get the attention of a dozen over-excited youngsters.

"Everyone! Ice-cream and cake will be later - over there," she said, indicating the food-tables on the other side of the veranda. "Then, if you are all good children, there will be presents for everyone later."

"We need games," William said.

"Later. Pin-the-tail-on-the-donkey: up here when it's dark. I suggest croquet for now."

"We'll need help out front," William said.

Emily bent down to speak to a nine year old in a blue jacket and small, round eye-glasses.

"Philip! Help get the others together for a game downstairs," she said, before she disappeared into the house, returning with Iris, a young black woman, outfitted in a blue uniform and Plimsolls. Once everyone had descended to the lawn, William and Iris had to shout above the excitement to organize the troop into four teams.

"Now listen to Iris when she speaks to you," William said, as Emily came to his side.

"Hilarious, William," she said, pointing to Sarah, a blond minuet whose mallet would not connect with a ball.

For William, the abandon with which she said his name was the ultimate exhilaration. At the same time he knew how quickly her mood could change and break the spell.

"Soon they will wonder what comes next," he said at last.

She smiled at him. "Maybe they would prefer rides on Dad's old bike. What do you think?"

William nodded in agreement. He could have suggested it himself, except that the idea coming from Emily was so much better. The crusty black bicycle, with a cross-bar suitable for a passenger, was in the shed beside the stables. Running as fast as he could, he set out to retrieve it, dreading that Emily would change her mind before he lowered the seat, put air in the tires, and wiped down the frame.

As he had anticipated, many of the younger ones had lost interest in croquet by the time he got back to the lawn and rang the bell on the handlebar.

"Everyone who wants to ride this flying-machine with me: line up, please."

First, the younger children with William gripping the seat from behind the bicycle and Iris beside the passenger on the bar. Then Philip and the older ones in turn, with William in the saddle. Finally, his big chance arrived.

"Emily, it's your turn now," he said, holding the bicycle with one arm extended and the other beckoning her to ride with him. Caught by surprise and a little embarrassed, Emily shook her head in protest. For a moment William wished he had not taken the risk.

Then, without further ado, she relented.

"Why not, you naughty boy," she said, as she swept shiny black hair into a loose knot, and hoisted herself unto the crossbar.

With the older ones cheering them on, William took off down the driveway, with Emily constantly off-balance on the cross-bar in front of him. At first he was speechless, enjoying his good fortune that was as unexpected as it was glorious. As they sped down the drive, he was suddenly conscious that Emily was enclosed within his arms. She had surrendered her safety to him.

When the wind blew her hair across his face, the smell of her perfume filled him with emotions he did not fully understand and thoughts he tried unsuccessfully to suppress. In wild abandon he was pedalling ever faster down the slope, when she rested her head against his. A lightning bolt that flashed before him, vividly revealing the future. He must ask her to marry him so that they could be together, always.

"Let's go back now, William."

"Already?"

"This bar hurts."

"We have to discuss something, Emily," William said. With a heavy heart he backed off the bicycle and held the seat in order to let her down.

"It's almost dark, and they are all waiting."

"Yes, of course," he said, disheartened, but at the same time elated that he would not have to face up to an answer, just yet.

"Cars are coming," she said. They were enveloped in dust from three vehicles returning from the polo-tournament conference. Without warning, she wrested the bicycle from William's grip and, laughing, took-off at a run up the driveway with it, steering the two-wheeler as best she could from the saddle.

Deflated in spirit, and not in a mood to confront her again, William trudged up the driveway, reaching the front lawn to discover that the children had been assembled on the veranda. Not seeing Emily among them and convinced she was avoiding him, he was already gathering up the crocket equipment scattered about on the lawn, when Iris came to tell him that everyone was waiting to see him upstairs.

Confidence restored and Emily forgiven, he bounded up the steps to the veranda, quickly checking that Iris had everything under control before he ran across the empty ballroom and found the entrance to the morning room. Inside was Emily, in the company of her father and several house guests whom William did not recognize, except for Emily's tall friend with the eyepatch. No one spoke as he entered, and Emily pretended not to see him. Then he realized she was sobbing and he understood the silence. To his surprise, she broke away from her father to stand beside him.

"Fisher was killed," she said in a whisper.

"He's dead?"

Robert Stroud, unsteady behind his daughter, came over to them. "Unfortunat'ly so, William. In a fight with Busha." The liquor was evident on his breath when he placed his hands on their shoulders and continued, "w'al' feel so bad seeing how poplar he was with you youngsters."

"He was here just a few days ago," William said, trying hard to make sense of the bad news. Fisher dead. This could not be. Delivering fish one day and dead the next? William had never seen a dead person; well, except Uncle Norman packed in ice at Rockwell. But no one *missed* him.

"Terrible, William," Mr. Stroud said, turning to include Mr. Thompson, who William saw was clean-cut, tall, and kindly-looking in spite of his intimidating eyewear.

"Why shoot Fisher?" Emily had stopped sniffling.

"Not shot, my dear," Mr. Thompson said.

"Complicated it is," her father hastened to add. "W' al will know the full story tomorrow," he continued, before turning to welcome his wife who had appeared in the doorway.

"Miriam, Love. We have been waiting for you."

William had never seen Emily's mother in this light before. It was not only her magisterial bearing that he noticed as she glided into the room, but also her strikingly slim legs and red high-heeled shoes, which, with her every step, were teasingly visible through the side-slits in her evening-dress.

"I had no idea you were waiting for me, my darlings," she said, bowing to the guests with a flourish. "I heard about the tragedy, and came to console the youngsters."

"The lady is gorgeous," Mr. Thompson said as he hugged Miriam Stroud around the waist.

"Of course, the children must be distraught at this terrible occurrence," she said. "But don't we also have to consider that Busha is the accused? What effect will this have on the matches? Is he not scheduled to referee the finals?"

William felt the world close in on him. Busha had killed Fisher. Was he, William Farnam, not an accomplice in his friend's death? He desperately wanted to be alone. Get away from all this stuff about polo matches he must. Having paid his respects he left Emily with her mother's arm around her and ran to the stables to fetch Chestnut.

Did he not know that Ralph had wished Busha dead for hurting Rajani? Why did Fisher get involved? And anyway, what difference did it make that Fisher got to Busha first, only to be killed himself? Ralph would have met the same fate. If in that case William's silence would have been culpable, why not now?

Never before had he been confronted with the death of a friend, let alone the responsibility for having stood by when he could have prevented it. In school, discussions about death were reserved for religion classes in which the end of human life was tied to God and the punishment of sinners. The unrepentant suffered Purgatory, or worse if in a state of mortal sin. Where had his inaction put Fisher?

On the morning after the terrible news broke, a telephone call from the police station interrupted William's breakfast with his mother. Norman Farnam, fresh out of bed and still in dressing gown and slippers, took the call, speaking with some deference to the caller. Although he seldom smoked before lunch, he was biting on an empty pipe when he joined them at the table.

"Busha is in custody. There was an altercation. He claims that Fisher was drunk and attacked him with a cleaver. He had to use his knife."

The gist of this they already knew from Ralph's account. Poor Fisher - he was murdered without a chance of confessing his sins, William thought. Yet he also knew there was something Ralph had kept to himself, someone Ralph was protecting and about whom not even the police were aware.

"Don't be so morose, William. Baptists don't have confession. Anyway, murder is for the court."

"They want me to identify the body, dear," Norman said.

Dorothy Farnam stopped preparing the tea. Reversing her wheelchair she turned and propelled it over to her husband's side of the breakfast table. "I couldn't do that, Norm."

"Don't worry, dear. I understand the Indian woman was present."

"Must have been a domestic quarrel," Dorothy Farnam said, as she moved back to the other side of the table to continue with the tea.

"Fisher doesn't have a family, mother," William said.

"He was her brother."

"Whose brother?"

"Matty - the Indian woman's. You must have known that, son" Norman Farnam said.

William was struck dumb. Of course! How ignorant could he have been not to connect Fisher with Matty? Finally, fearful of more questions when he saw his father's face light up, he said: "I didn't know about Matty."

"Did you not see her a few days ago?"

"Only very briefly, father."

"And her daughter?"

"She was sick, as you told me."

"Well, we will learn more about this at the hearing. It is set for next Tuesday, I understand," Norman Farnam said.

Relieved that his father did not pursue the issue, William sank back in his chair, almost happy to wait for the hearing.

It came and went. William learned from his father that Hopeview Estate's magnates in England had provided the barrister to represent Busha. The coroner accepted the position that Fisher had a temper, and, that an argument, which somehow involved

Matty, had resulted in his attacking Busha with criminal intent. He ruled the stabbing death not indictable, leaving the community to return to normal.

Set for next week Saturday, Fisher's funeral could not have been better planned to upset William. He very much wanted to be there, especially as his father would have to go in place of Ralph, who was still laid up because of his back. But next Saturday was the day of Emily's party.

The ache in having to miss the celebration was made worse by the persistent sense of remorse for his not telling someone about Rajani's condition. He tried to console himself by dismissing as too vague what he thought she said about Busha.

In the end, he steeled himself and visited Ralph to demand a full explanation of what Rajani had told him, and why he wished Busha dead. To no avail. Ralph said his comment had meant nothing; that the matter was best left alone. William swore to keep everything a secret.

Saturday afternoon found William resigned to missing Emily's party.

"We're supposed to be in Falmouth by 4:00P.M.," Norman Farnam said, as he squeezed his ample torso into the narrow front seat of the Morris Minor. The first leg of their journey lay ahead.

Even though the highway bordered the sea and the sun was off its peak, their progress west was hot and sticky. Their only cooling was the wind through the open car windows - not enough for the protracted waits *en route.* Ancient country busses topped with crocus bags and suitcases, and aggressively driven bauxite trucks, brought them to repeated halts on the narrow highway. William's plan to wonder through Falmouth market, maybe to visit the fishing village where his friend grew up, quickly faded.

Brown's Funeral Home was on a back road lined with ramshackle buildings wearing corrugated zinc roofs coated in varying shades of red. The wooden building was the only one containing a second floor with a latticed balcony. The main entrance to the chapel opened on to an adjoining lot where a small crowd had gathered around a hearse.

"That's Fisher's sister, Matty, beside his widow and two sons." Norman Farnam observed as they left the car and crossed the street. "His father must be inside. So far, no Rajani."

A short black man, with powder-puffs on his jacket, stood guard over the hearse, the back doors of which were open. Most of the mourners were men. It struck William that many of them would have come from the village. Of the small number of women, two were dressed in ankle-length black gowns and head scarves. Matty was consoling Fisher's wife, who, flanked by her two teenage boys, was weeping openly.

"Sanjay is in dark glasses," William said, pointing out Fisher's brother. The last thing he wanted was to be drawn into a discussion about the women.

They joined the crowd around the hearse just as a tall black man, dressed in a dark three-piece suit, appeared in the doorway of the funeral home. After introducing himself as Reverend Brown he invited everyone to enter. At the door, the man with the powder-puffs came over to them and suggested they join the family at the front of the room. William wanted to do so, but his father politely declined. The crowd grew in size and the room got hotter.

William had difficulty seeing around mourners who were blocking his view of the coffin that lay open on a trolley. He had only glimpses of Fisher's body enfolded in white. Behind the trolley stood a metal cross on a wooden base, and beside it, a podium on which rested a large, leather-bound bible. Out of place beside the trolley was a man with a mop of grey hair, who clutched to his chest a black book of his own, as if it gave him confidence to move the trolley back and forth without finding the best spot for it.

"That's Fisher's father, from Kempshot," Norman Farnam said. "His mother is dead."

With no introduction a piano began pounding out "Rock of Ages" and everyone was upstanding in song. Reverend Brown's address followed. His sonorous invocation filled the room. Caught unawares by the emotions swelling up around him, William tried hard to preserve self-control.

Rishita Karmari, also known as "Fisher," had forbears who, more than a century before, came to Trelawney as indentured labour from northern India. Like them, Fisher's parents lived in poverty and expected him as a youth to help feed his siblings. The result was he served two
years hard labour for stealing a goat.

William heard what was said, without his emotions getting the better of him, that is, until Reverend Brown spoke of Fisher's generosity in sharing what little he had with others, young and old, that he suddenly was overcome. He paid little attention to the rest of the service. Only after the pallbearers deposited the coffin in the hearse and closed the doors behind it did he fully realize he would never again see his friend alive.

The motorcade that accompanied the hearse consisted of an old bus, and a rusted truck with an open back fitted with metal chairs for the passengers. William and his father were behind the truck, their Morris Minor hiccupping through Falmouth's crowded streets before turning south into the interior. The gravel road was narrow, and because of the other vehicles ahead, it soon became very dusty in the car.

"It's going to be hotter, but roll up the windows please," Norman Farnam said. "I hope we get to Kempshot before we bake or choke to death."

"Fisher was not a Maroon, father."

"No. Only Ralph claims to be a descendent."

"So why are Fisher's family from around Cockpit Country?"

"As you heard, his forebears made their home in these parts."

"I don't understand."

"Again, they came as indentured labour."

"What's that?"

"After Emancipation, the slaves from Africa deserted the estates. East Indian and Chinese labourers were recruited to work in the fields for stated periods."

"Did Rockwell employ any?"

"No idea. That was a hundred and twenty years ago. Granddad Farnam bought Rockwell in 1925."

"Fisher once told me about reincar--"

"Reincarnation. Returning, after death."

"In another body?"

"Yes."

"Or as an animal, or a bird?"

"Yes, maybe."

"Fisher told me his ancestors believed that," William said "He converted to Christianity when he was in prison."

"So why did they not go back to India?"

"Jamaicans all came from elsewhere, son. Everyone here was a stranger in a strange land at some point in our history."

The idea had never occurred to William. "Just like Emily?"

"Exactly. Some early, some later."

"She is my best friend."

"We like her too, William."

"I wish I was at her birthday party. I really wanted to go, father."

"You're doing the right thing, William. Many more parties to come, son."

The dusty road was narrow and winding. They were forced to slow to a crawl in order to let oncoming vehicles get past. In the lower and drier areas, the fields were planted in coconut. As they climbed into the interior these gave way to swaths of pasture land, partitioned by stone fences and enclosing sheep, or, more often, horned cattle accompanied by winged friends. Quite often, they left in the dust women carrying firewood on their heads; occasionally, an empty fruit-shelter accommodating half-naked youths at play.

"Such large stomachs," William said.

"Too many starches."

"Because they are poor?"

"Unfortunately."

"That's not fair, father. What about the poor people on Rockwell?"

"Life is not fair, William."

"Slavery was not."

"Certainly not. Very bad time for the great majority in this country. But they survived, and taught the estate owners a lesson in refusing to work for them."

"Ralph says that one hundred and fifty years ago, after a big rebellion, many of his people were captured and executed.

"There were many revolts."

"He says that in the Great Maroon War, there were executions using terrible torture. One Maroon prisoner was tied, sitting on the ground, and burned: his feet first, then up his legs, then up.... And yet he never screamed, not once."

"I believe that's true."

"After that, many of the prisoners were shipped to Canada."

"Nova Scotia, I believe."

After climbing for some time, the procession came to an abrupt halt before a concrete building wedged into the side of the hill. Fisher's brother, Sanjey, jumped off the bus and disappeared within the cramped structure. Minutes later he emerged with two bottles, one of which he passed up to passengers in the bus through a side window.

Still climbing, the procession reached Kempshot, and finally the family's piece of ground beside a shallow gully. William held onto his father as the party followed the pastor and the pallbearers down the incline, across water at the bottom of it, and up the other side.

"Fisher work us out good," said one.

"Him not coming back from this place," said another.

The plateau at the top was thick in grass and the air sprinkled with the smell of wild flowers. Laying across a freshly dug grave were two planks, upon which the pallbearers set the casket. A gasp went up when the pastor lifted the cover to reveal a white cloud rising about the body.

"From the dry-ice keeping him cool," Norman Farnam said.

Seeing Fisher up close, William was struck by his dead friend's pasty skin, the manicured finger nails, and bushy eyebrows he had never noticed before.

"That's him. The same Fisher," one woman said, and the sentiment was repeated as the mourners circled Fisher's well dressed torso.

"Him more hansom than before," another woman said, holding her hat as she leaned over the casket to get a closer look.

In turn, Matty bent over the coffin, gesticulating and talking to the waxen figure imploringly: "Remember we sufferers from up there, brother."

Fisher's father, still holding his book, stood some distance from the grave. He seemed nervous as he wiped his face with a purple handkerchief until Sanjey led him over to the coffin. Once there, he opened the book and in halting tones read passages which condemned violence and spoke of an eternal soul. What struck William as profound was the one proclaiming that, even after it is killed, the body will wear new clothes in the next world.

"What is the name of that book, father?"

"The Bagavad, or Bagavita, I believe it is. Hindu holy book."

"Their bible?"

"Something like that."

When his father could not continue, Sanjey joined him beside the casket and they agreed on something, before the younger one produced from his coat pocket the bottle he had acquired earlier. Holding it up for all to see, he then ceremoniously slipped it down the inside of the casket to the loud approval of everyone.

"You can rest easy now, Brother. This is for celebration," he said, stroking the waxed figure once more, before securing the lid.

The casket was lowered into the grave while the closing hymn echoed throughout the canyon in competition with barefoot youths wheeling and turning cement. Their rasping shovels were no match for the Rock of Ages.

Emily was half-hiding her face behind her hair as she stood in the middle of the driveway. "I will never forgive you," she said haughtily. Her green blouse over tight white shorts made a statement William appreciated without fully understanding. All of a sudden, she looked older. Could it be the low neckline, or maybe the tone of voice – gamely threatening as usual, yet unusually apologetic at the same time?

"That's not fair," William said, dismounting from Chestnut.

"It is so. You were specially invited."

He realized she was pleading with him.

"I saw Fisher's body. In a casket."

Emily's expression changed from feigned anger, to regret.

"Forgive me, William. I forgot about that."

"I brought this for your birthday," he said, producing the present his mother had chosen.

"*Great Expectations*. I can't wait!" Emily said, hugging the book and sneaking over to kiss him on the cheek. "You're an angel."

Taken by surprise, William could only fiddle with Chestnut's reins.

"I must tie him up."

"Yes, dummy. It's a lovely afternoon for a walk."

"Really?"

"And I have lots of leftovers. Go tether that animal of yours," she said; and, as she turned to go up the front steps, continued in a matter of fact invitation, "we'll have a picnic."

William could hardly believe his ears. Never had they gone on a picnic. Was this not the chance of a lifetime to tell her of his love? Pulling on the reins, he ran with Chestnut to the stables, found him a stall, and, out of breath and heart pounding, returned to wait for Emily.

When she reappeared, she had a basket with sandwiches, a bottle of orange juice, and a table cloth tucked in beside the novel. She seemed excited about something, but William did not have the courage to ask why.

"I say the polo ground. You choose the spot," she said, handing him the basket. Without waiting for a response, she led the way across the front lawn, crocket goals in place, and then down the rough-stone steps to the polo field, replete with heaps of freshly cut grass on its boundary line.

"By the mound behind the goal posts - under the tree," she said, pointing to the yellow Poui in the distance. "The blooms will be gone in two days."

"Catch me, then," William said, racing off ahead, with Emily trying to keep up. Reaching the tree first he threw himself unto the butter-colour carpet beneath it.

"Okay Great One. The cloth, please," she said. Out of breath, and perspiring from heat and exertion, they both went for the orange juice.

"We'll have to share it," William said.

"Your turn. You are the guest."

"I'll settle for a sandwich too," he said, sipping the orange juice before handing it over. "Tell me about the party."

"So much to tell!"

"How many came?"

"Some of my girlfriends came for the day. The formalities did not begin until 5:30 - with cocktails, of course. About forty for dinner - toasts to me and all, followed by a huge cake that Iris and the kitchen baked. Then music and dancing. Just imagine what you missed. The ballroom was packed! School friends, as well as the older people, of course, were all decked out in their fineries. The Suttons came from Kingston, Marleys from Black River, and on, and on. I wore a new green off-the-shoulder dress with a daring neckline. Can you just see me in it?"

"Must have looked like a movie star."

"First off, I danced with Daddy. In black tie, he was. I also danced a waltz with Mr. Thompson. You know…"

"Was his wife there?"

"She's in Canada. I'd been trying to charm him into telling me about my parents' life in England during the war. No luck. He just smiles, just as they do when I ask them – all mysterious like."

William was trying not to look down her blouse. "I have something to tell you."

"Then, I danced with young Arnold Mantovan, son of that bauxite man from Mandeville, and David Brandon from Montego Bay, and on and on. Just super."

"I have something to tell you, Emily."

"Anyway, everyone loved the banquet."

"Yes, but…."

"Fresh salmon delivered the day before by Fisher's son."

"Sanjey was there. At the funeral, I mean."

"And then, the steaks from Hopeview Estate."

"You mean?"

"Slaughtered for the party. The meat was specially aged."

"I didn't know… I wanted to tell you about that."

"Something else to tell me? Have another sip," she said, drinking of the orange juice before she passed the bottle to him. Drinking after her, he could see she was amused at his shyness. Why should he mind? He was too happy to care about anything else if she was by his side.

"We're like priests co-celebrating mass," he said.

"Is that what Jesuits do?"

"Sometimes."

"They wouldn't do what we girls did…."

"Something bad?"

"Not really….Well, a little, maybe."

"Tell me, tell me, Emily."

"We played spin-the-bottle – me, Sandy, Marge, and three others…"

"At the party?"

"Of course not. We spent the day together doing things, you know, even practicing the love-making."

"As in the movies?"

"Sort of."

"Really?"

"Deep-kissing an' all."

"Ugh…I suppose you won't go to confession."

"We were experimenting, dummy. Just for fun!"

Stupid, stupid – how stupid could he be? She was asking him to kiss her, was she not? He wanted to, so much. The idea was almost too tantalising to contemplate. There she sat: composed, pouting, but oblivious of the moral strictures that plagued him.

"I have something to tell you, Emily."

She half-turned and looked at him with mischievous eyes.

"Remember. You're addressing a woman now."

"Really…?"

"Yes. *It* began - at last."

"What do you mean?"

"My period. During school, before Christmas would you believe? Kept it a secret for a while, or so I thought. Finally told mother. She said she already knew! I'm all grown-up, she said."

"I see."

"No, you don't. One day, I'll explain."

"Explain what, Emily?"

"I've changed from a girl to a woman, mother says. From cute worm to butterfly. So there!"

"Tell me what…."

"It's too private."

"I can ask mother."

"I prefer you didn't."

"Then, tell me what's happened."

The colour rose in her cheeks as she explained her condition. The icy-cold of a few minutes ago had melted. Now she was vulnerable, trusting him with her secret as she had trusted him with her body on the bicycle. Much of what she said made no sense, but it didn't matter. He was enjoying the company of a confessional Emily sitting by his side among the blossoms.

"I hope it doesn't hurt," he said, having decided this was not a discussion for his mother.

"You were telling me about Fisher."

"Yes. I knew someone would die, and I said nothing."

"Meaning what, William?"

"Remember Rajani? I saw her. Badly beaten, she was."

"Oh?"

"What you just said about women and babies. The bundle, all bloody, was in a corner. Ralph said he would kill the man."

"Awful, William. But Ralph didn't kill anyone, did he?"

"No."

"Then stop blaming yourself."

"Fisher was killed instead, don't you see?"

"Stop worrying," she said as she reached over to him.

Without thinking, he leaned toward her at the same time and found himself enmeshed in her hair. Suddenly he was aware of the closeness of her bare legs, with bare feet tucked under them.

"I always liked your feet, Emily."

"You are a strange boy, you are." She allowed a foot to peek out and wave at him from beneath a thigh.

"Can I hold it?"

"Go ahead, if you must, dummy."

Summoning up the courage to do so, he gently traced with his thumb the curve of her instep. "It's small and delicate, but strong too."

"That tickles," she said, withdrawing her foot.

"Mother says *Great Expectations* was not regarded as one of Dickens' greatest books, until after he died."

"Is she very sick now?"

"Just weak. She could be in an iron lung."

"Makes her even more special. Like mother is for me, always watching over me so lovingly."

"You won't listen to what I have to tell you, Emily."

"I thought you told me." Sitting upright and brushing off petals that had fallen on her from the branches above, she was not as close to him as she had been. "You are invited to the tournament this weekend. Father would be happy for me if you came. He likes you a lot."

"I can't come. Busha will be there."

"That again. I want to see you before I leave."

Leave? The possibility had never occurred to him.

"To go where, Emily?"

"To attend high school, study French. In Montreal, no less."

"You never told me. Why not?"

"As well as a birthday party, this was a surprise farewell party. Early next month, I'll be attending what's called the Fall Semester."

His world was in tatters. "Why are you doing this?"

"It's all about to change, William. Father says the politics are turning against us in Jamaica. Something about independence from England this summer. Many of our friends are uncertain about the future, aren't your mom and dad?"

"Never heard them mention it."

Without warning the moment for declaring his love was slipping out of reach, beyond his ability to retrieve it.

"Mine don't plan to leave, not tomorrow anyhow," she said, scolding him for needing so much assurance. "You know my dad. He thinks too much about his horses. He's on a buying spree in Miami right now! Not for him to be packing suitcases just yet."

"And your mother?"

"She will wait and see. Wants to expand the resort properties. Also plans to put a thousand acres into pimento, here at Stroud Hall. Says the future is in Pimento oil - for making perfume."

"So, please, say you'll stay also."

"You don't understand, William: I'll be home for holidays."

His confidence returning, he stood up and surveyed the polo field that had been partially shielded from view by the mound of cut-grass.

"I wish I could be here for the big event," he said. "Someday, I'll ride in a tournament myself."

The time had arrived, right that minute, before he lost his nerve yet again. He must declare his great love, the love he had felt for her ever since he first saw her years ago, but especially since last Thursday, when his arms had enfolded her. He knew then he had to put aside fears of rejection and humiliation; tell her how he felt about her before someone else did; ask her to marry him, and accept her reply with grace.

"A foot is just a foot, William. This is the real thing."

Her words were distinctively seductive. He turned around to see that she had unbuttoned her blouse, revealing a breast nestled in its folds. Head held high she sat very still, looking with detachment into the distance. He tried to speak, but was overcome with wonder, transfixed by alluring womanhood that beckoned and terrified him at the same time.

"Look. Don't touch

Unable to do otherwise he whispered, "Thanks, Emily."

"Just so that you will remember me when we are both old and married - to other people of course," she said as she covered herself with a flourish. "And don't forget - you had something to tell me."

"Yes. Oh yes, I did."

"So?"

"It's not important."

"So, tell me anyway."

"I wanted you to know…."

"Go on, dummy,"

"I just wanted to tell you that I am not going to kill any more birds, Emily. Not ever."

CHRISTMAS STOCKING

1973

Looking into the brightly lit store window, Albert Grant reached without thinking for the bottle in his back pocket, removed the cap, and took a lingering swallow. The almost pure alcohol seared his throat, setting up a tingling in his chest walls. He replaced the cap, and eased the bottle into his pocket once more. A white mannequin in a low-cut swimsuit looked out onto the deserted plaza from behind the glass of Madame Boutique. A black one was equally curvaceous in short shorts and side-shoulder blouse. The sign between them said "Merry Christmas".

Further down the mall, Albert shone his light down the alley beside the department store before stopping at a window displaying a Christmas tree bedecked in plastic icicles and cotton snow. In front were trucks in assorted colours, a rocking-horse, and a red wagon with a pull handle. What the toys lacked in variety they made up in solid construction. The wagon would be nice for the two younger boys, he thought, if only he could afford it.

Buttoning the neck of his uniform to ward off the chill of the December night, he moved on. The Christmas tree lights cast an amber glow onto the sidewalk. He could feel the rum going to his head, and decided he would take a break at the end of this round. Before that, maybe he would smoke one of the joints he had saved from last night. The alternative was for him to relax until midnight, then, after a good rest, to kick off the next round. His pace quickened. He passed the beauty salon without looking in, and the bank into which he momentarily shone his flashlight.

Next, there was the small grass divide with a cut-stone fountain and concrete benches in front of it. Instead of crossing to the stores on the other side, he slipped the baton out of its holster on his leg, turned left at the end of the block, and walked up behind the buildings. Soon, he found he had retraced his steps past the mannequins, the toys, the beauty salon…

"Beg you someting for Christmas, sar."

The boy, not more than fifteen, was tall and dirty. His open khaki shirt revealed protruding ribs. One pant-leg was torn and jagged above the knee, while the other flapped around a bare foot. In the shadows, lurked two or three companions - younger maybe, fearful surely, moths attracted to light - waiting for a favourable reaction before coming forward.

Albert Grant ignored the youth, slapping his baton threateningly against his thigh. The youngster shrunk into the shadows, and immediately reappeared.

"Me 'ungry too!" He said, with a wary eye on the stick.

"Here. Take it and go home," Albert said

"Me too," a companion said.

The youth beamed as he ran forward to grab the coin. Two other straggling forms emerged from the shadows, but Albert paid no attention to them, adjusting the .38 on his hip for emphasis. He crossed the open area that boasted the fountain, then, realizing that the spotlights illuminating it had been left on by mistake, he stopped to make a note in his log.

He found himself in front of Wong's Travel where, in the window, a '707' was poised in flight. The banner above the cut away showing the interior of the plane said *Fly us for Christmas*. Another large poster proclaimed *Five flights a day to Miami*. He had been to Miami, once, on a training program. He remembered the trip and the small plane; and terror when they ran into bad weather over Cuba and had to make an unscheduled stop in Santa Clara. He recalled the oppressive heat of the Florida summer, the many big cars, and the rich flavour of the city. Never had he seen so many things to buy, with so little money in his pocket. White people were everywhere and not very approachable, but still he had hated to leave. Except for an empty wallet, he would have remained behind and disappeared, as many of his friends had done over the years.

One day he would return, he thought. There, an experienced man could find work, provided he was a hustler and able to stay out of the jaws of U.S. Immigration. Even the under-the-table money was good. One could sport a woman on it, and still have a bit left over at the end of a month.

He gazed into the window for some time, obsessively spinning the baton by means of the strap wrapped around his wrist. His daydream was over when he reached again for the bottle in his back pocket. This time the hit was less than before. He let the empty bottle fall to the pavement and, as expected, one of the moth-like creatures fluttered out of the dark to retrieve it.

Some distance away, a sound system began to pound out music that drifted across on the night air in waves of loud and soft. He decided he would take a break. Maybe half an hour at Morgan's Place would put him in a better mood. His steps became purposeful as he turned and made his way across the deserted plaza towards the road, on the other side of which, a short distance away, he could not help seeing the familiar neon sign.

All he had on him was $5.00 and some change. After the bus fare, this would leave him $4.20. Then, of course, there were tomorrow's fares to think about, and the prospect of a whole night's work without a drink. Maybe he should wait, and buy a bottle tomorrow night. His pace slowed, but he did not stop and turn back. The urgency with which he had advanced, almost to the street, could not be overcome entirely by monetary considerations for the morrow.

It was quite busy for this time of night. The cinema, two doors up the road, had just let out - evidenced by a staccato of car-doors and shouts on the night air. As he approached the south entrance of the mall, he heard the clatter before he saw 'Scarecrow' returning from one of his frequent sorties. Stooped under his possessions, his knotty frame was covered by the remnants of a raincoat.

Almost doubled over, with arms outstretched, he clutched a stick in each hand to support his back, across which, pressing him ever closer to the ground, was a tightly rolled bundle that passed for a mattress. From around his waist, suspended by a string, was a clutch of tin cans. And yet, the entertainment he provided, especially for children, came not only from the din and clatter of metal on metal - accompanied by grunts and groans, as from his precarious walk. He was everyone's ultimate absurdity whose every step could be his last.

Tonight, the human tortoise was blabbering to himself in an unbroken stream of nothings as he arrived outside 'Teen Town Fashions', crawled into a sitting position on a piece of cardboard against the wall, and busied himself buttoning his fly.

"Is night, now," Albert shouted. "Don't harass yourself walking back and forth."

The blabbering stopped momentarily. The heap on the mat looked up with the vacant expression of one who cannot see.

Albert demonstrated with his fingers, to no avail. Then he bent closer: "Use one of the tins, old fool."

The heap strained to say something, but only made guttural noises in reply.

"Mad as hell," Albert said.

One morning he had seen Scarecrow running the gauntlet of four school children. Apparently, they were testing the theory that he was a fake. The sport was to try to take away his sticks, in order to see if he could stand up without them. Scarecrow had been ready for them that morning, and proceeded to beat off their advances with one stick, while supporting himself with the other.

Soon, a small crowd of onlookers had gathered to witness the drama. Some scolded the attackers, others shouted at Scarecrow to protect his rear. The three boys and a girl split up and, while their victim struck out at two of them in front, the other two attempted to trip him from behind. Scarecrow's face was soon contorted. His blabbering became screeches and he was drooling from his mouth. It certainly made for a good laugh when he was provoked, Albert remembered. What thrilled the crowd most were the occasions when an attacker got too close at the wrong moment, and a heavy stick came into full contact with a retreating rump. Then the shout went up:

"Whip them again, Scarecrow, and make we see it."

Albert had stopped to admonish Scarecrow, but the neon sign on the other side of the road continued to beckon him on. He could see two women in tight skirts strolling under the lights as he rounded the entrance of the plaza, where two children pushing a peanut cart with a loud steam-whistle, overtook him. He stopped them and purchased a 30 cent bag.

"You no go home at night?"

The question was directed at the younger one, now clearly a girl of about ten years old. She only smiled, with a vacant look on her face. Deaf, he thought, opening the bag and selecting a large three-holler. The husk was hot, the kernels stale. He could have demanded another packet, but the whistle was already wheeling down the road, vapour enveloping two heads bent over the pushing-handle.

He contented himself by cracking shells one at a time as he walked, extending an arm above his head to pop the nuts into his mouth. It took only a few minutes for him to cover the twelve hundred feet of road frontage opposite Morgan's, by which time he was thirsty.

There was no question he needed a drink now, not tomorrow, or any other time. The traffic had thinned to a trickle. As he crossed the street, a clock-tower in the vicinity struck midnight. He was behind schedule. In front of the Morgan's Place he found his way barred.

"We thirsty too, Babe," the one with the big bottom said to him in a feigned American accent.

He brushed by the women and entered the building by the side door. The near empty lounge with its sturdy wooden chairs and tables was quite large. Several Christmas streamers, suspended from the ceiling, had lost their wall moorings and lay partly on, partly off, the dance floor, on the left side of which four couples shuffled listlessly to music from a Juke Box. On the right was a semi-circular bar and a number of alcoves housing red couches and tables covered with Christmas paper. At the back of the room, a raised and acoustically curved bandstand with ornate carvings gave a hint of better days.

"You running late tonight, Mr. Al," the woman behind the bar said. Hers was a crude youthfulness, round of face and rounder of hip, boasting straightened hair and painted finger nails.

He went to the end of the counter, and called to her softly:

"Is pay day for me tomorrow, Miss Agatha."

"You go on," she said, taking time to wipe the counter in front of him.

"Make us do a thing, nah?" He said, gazing at half-covered bosoms.

"But you work tomorrow night," she said, turning away with a sheepish smile.

"Can arrange it, sister." He caught hold of her wrist and pulled her closer. "Make we go dance. And…"

"And then what? You too brazen. What you want to drink?"

He fumbled in his pocket for the loose change he knew he had.

"Squeeze me one," he said, offering her what he found.

"For only fifty cents?"

"All I can afford," he said, without results. "Them youth in the plaza took some. Pour a half, then."

"You good at heart," Agatha said, glancing cautiously in the direction of the barman before ringing in the money and returning with the glass.

"So what 'bout it?"

"I work tomorrow," she said, without conviction.

"Look, Miss Agatha," he said, leaning over the counter. "Man and woman born to groove. We made for each other. How anyone to know we not just go dance tomorrow?"

"That was before your troubles, and my work, Mr. Al. Now is different."

His face fell. She was playing with him and scolding him at the same time.

"Since when you work on Fridays? Is lie you lying to me, sister...?"

Half smiling she ignored him. Moving to the other side of the counter she began serving a man wearing a ball-cap.

"Cha, you run joke now," Albert said, almost to himself as he looked at his watch and realized he had little time to rest before the end of his shift. In a few hours he was due up at Jack's Hill to chauffer the Lawrence children and could not risk smelling of liquor. "I too tired to fight with you."

Someone punched a number and the Juke Box spoke directly to Albert ...*IMF want to starve black man... starve black man an' him women an' chil'ren....*

Agatha had returned to his side of the bar and, with an eye on the barman, deftly replaced Albert's empty glass with a full one.

"Heard she back from hospital," she said.

"Yes, at home since last week."

"What did doctor say about it?"

"Same sugar that kill her brother. The medcine expensive and she distress herself too much," he said, sipping on the glass as he remembered how good his wife used to look.

Tonight he had left her weak and distraught. Two years ago he saw his brother-in-law deteriorate from a big-framed, strong man, into a bed-ridden skeleton, because he could not afford the recommended diet, let alone the prescription that the hospital said was his only hope. Now, his wife's turn had come. In her condition, she could no longer cope. The two boys were missing school and his form of discipline was not working.

"How come you so quiet, man?" She asked, touching his arm.

"Had to strap one of them today."

"Is what you say?"

"Nothing."

He remembered the incident that afternoon. He had taken the strap to Nevil on the veranda of their home, which was situated on a lane behind an office building. The boy had buried his face between his knees in order to ward off the blows directed at his back and shoulders.

Albert recalled that when the boy's cries reached a peak a brown-skin man in a business-suit had emerged unto the back porch of the office building across the divide. This man had stood quite still, staring intently at him as he continued to administer the punishment. That is, until he could not raise his arm to the boy while the man looked on. Only then did the man leave the porch.

"You gone quiet on me," Agatha said.

He felt she was warming to him. Except that now he had no more time to pursue the matter. He drained the glass, and with some reluctance got up from the stool.

"You too sometimish, woman. Lend me a napkin."

She seemed not to hear; instead, she tried to get his attention as he turned to leave.

"Ten, tomorrow night?"

"Maybe not."

She spirited him the napkin. "So, where you goin' so soon?

"Miami, sister."

The street-women had gone. There were fewer cars on the road. The distant street music that earlier had been audible, was quieter now. Maybe the wind had changed, or maybe the police had intervened. Scarecrow was asleep on the cardboard, his mouth open, his two sticks across the sidewalk, so that Albert had to step off the walkway to get around them.

Three and a half hours left, he thought, looking at his watch. He decided to do just one more round before taking a rest. The walk took him by way of the east boundary, going past the hardware store and the supermarket, towards the alcove decorated with dwarf coconut.

This area was dominated by the shell of a large jewellery store that had been locked up since gunmen killed its proprietor. Except for three busts covered in black velvet, the showcases were empty. With his flashlight arching from left to right through the iron grillwork, Albert illuminated the cell-like interior, then inspected the chain securing the two front doors. Satisfied with the jewellery store, he made his way to the pharmacy, then around the perimeter of the alcove, where he repeated the inspection process through shop windows, ending up in the main plaza where he began. Noises close-by told him Morgan's was shutting down for the night.

A ticket would cost a lot of money. That much he knew: maybe two hundred dollars or more. It would have to be a return ticket too, or else they wouldn't allow him on the plane. It would take him three months to save that much - if he denied himself everything. The prospect of leaving behind this hand-to-mouth existence, of working for real money instead of JA dollars, appealed to him.

Life in a rich country was what he wanted. Why had he not made plans for that years ago? Yes, the worst could happen to spoil his fun. The solution was to find a woman with money as soon as he arrived. Surely, that would be easier to do than finding one here. So many black women with real dollars in Miami, and all of them speaking English. At the same time, a Common Law arrangement, such as he had now, would not be enough. The relationship would have to be legal if, in a worst-case scenario, he was faced with deportation.

Of course, there was good reason for him to think in these terms. For, unless he could find enough money to send back here, his baby-mother would die - just as her brother had died; and his boys would come to no good. Only in the US could he earn enough to avoid imminent disaster, of one kind or another, at home. Thus heartened, he decided he must start saving without delay.

Suddenly he was very tired. With several tours of the compound under his belt, he decided to stop and rest out of sight of prying eyes in the alley beside the department store. He spread the napkin on the concrete and made himself as comfortable as possible. Across the plaza from him Scarecrow was sprawled out on his mattress. Except for his inert frame the place was deserted. Leaning against the store wall, Albert Grant dozed off.

He had been asleep for some time, when he awoke with a start and anxiously looked around, expecting to see someone or something. But there was no movement in the plaza, and no sound except for the faint trickling of the fountain at the far end. The silence told him this was "duppy-hour", when wondering spirits were supposed to pass overhead on their way back to the graveyards.

This was the time of night he wished not to be disturbed. He sat listening for something to explain his sudden unease: a stray dog maybe, a car horn, anything except what he actually heard. The footsteps varied from faint to quite loud, as if soft then hard shoes were involved. Still sleep-deprived he was not sure of the their origin until the front door of the department store beside him rattled. Someone was trying to open it from the inside.

Drawing up his legs, he pressed himself against the wall and crept, below window-level, towards the door, at the same time slipping the .38 out of its holster and pulling back the hammer. There was no telling how many were in the store, or how well they were armed. The centre-piece of his training was: Do not go up against more than one gun. Sweat was running cold down his spine, as the door opened, and a head emerged, followed by a body on hands and knees pulling a plastic bag.

"Hold it right there," Albert commanded, still pressed against the wall for protection from anyone else in the store. He pointed with his gun. "Put it on the ground."

"Is nothing. Doan' shoot, sar ."

A barefoot boy no older than fifteen years stood up, dropping the bag as he did so.

"In the air, against the wall, you little rass."

"Let me go. Please, mister - is Christmas you know."

The boy seemed very afraid, but Albert wasn't taking any chances.

"You alone?"

"Yes, sar."

"On the wall, I said."

Holding the gun against a wiry head Albert frisked the youth and found a hacksaw blade in his pocket. Suddenly he recognized the shoeless intruder as the moth-like creature who had approached him earlier.

"What you got there?"

"Only someting to wear. See here, sar."

Albert looked incredulously at the two pairs of socks, and a pair of running shoes in a gift box.

"Leave it there, you little thief," he said as forcefully as he could. "Walk over to the phone and don't make any sudden moves."

"Please, misser. Me no do it again. Doan' make them come for me."

Holding the boy by the neck, Albert ignored the plea. He realized only too well he would have no job tomorrow if it could be construed that the store had been broken into when he was over at Morgan's, or worse when he was asleep. Holding the culprit was his only insurance.

"The phone, straight ahead," he barked, as he propelled the cringing frame towards the phone booth in front of the boutique.

The person on the other end of the line sounded tired. Yes, a squad car would be sent out to the plaza immediately. Albert put down the phone. Already he could see how, with a few embellishments, the story could be slanted in his favour.

"Soon be here," Albert said.

The boy pulled away at the news, then covered his face as Albert raised the gun to his head.

"Don't try anything, you little shit."

"Mi mother. She going beat me if she hear them come take me away."

Albert laughed. "Your mother? You won't see her for a while. Don't you know you can get two years for shop-lifting? This damn city is full of criminals like you."

"Me no criminal. Me just want some socks for Christmas. Believe me, sar."

The frightened youth half twisted round, in spite of the iron hold on his neck, and tried to look at his captor so that he began choking under Albert's grip.

"You little rass - want me whip you, right now?"

"Doan', doan' hit me, sar."

A glancing blow, the gun hand brushing the side of the head. The boy screamed, more from fright than pain, the sound bouncing off concrete and asphalt.

"You going to shut up?"

"No make them take me away."

"If you was my own son you would get more than a slap around the ear," Albert said, by way of justification. For a fleeting moment he remembered a bruised young face and outstretched arms, and the man gazing at him from across the way.

"You little shits are all the same."

The boy did not reply, just stood there, protecting his face with both hands.

"Can't be kind to you little shits," Albert continued. "Tonight you come beg. I give you money. Think you can make a fool out of me?"

"I no do that, sar. You can tek back the things now," the boy said, attempting to reach for the bag on the ground.

Albert drew him up straight and whispered in his ear.

"Where is your friends?"

"Gone 'ome."

"You stayed back all alone, eh?"

"Yes, sar. I no lie to you."

"You want me to slap you again?"

"No, no, sar."

"Sit down, and don't try anything."

Released, the youth stumbled onto the sidewalk and began rubbing his neck. In the half-light Albert could see sores on the thin arms that protruded from under the rags. "Why you didn't go home with the others?"

The youth hesitated. "Me no have nowhere to go."

"Don't lie to me. What about your mother?"

"Is truth I tell. She with anodder man."

"So?"

"Him no like me. The others - them have yard to go to."

It was clear that appeals to his domestic predicament gave the youth hope for this one.

Albert was less hopeful. "You'll have a new yard, from tonight." He saw the tears. There was something about the cowering figure in front of him that made him feel uncomfortable. The sunken, frightened stare was telling him a story he knew very well. Where were his boys at this moment? What stood between them and laws that jailed only poor people. He could save this boy from that eventuality. But what about his job?

The silence of the night was broken by the roar of a heavy vehicle travelling fast and turning into the gravel entrance of the plaza. The police jeep sped round to where they were, and two black men jumped out. One was Asian in appearance, clean shaven, with a red tam pulled down over his ears. He carried a flashlight, and wore a revolver on his hip. The other was unshaven, with dreadlocks and a goatee, and a rifle over his shoulder. Neither was in uniform. The clean-shaven man approached Albert and flashed a card.

"Special squad," he said, taking in the scene with a sweeping glance that excluded the youth on the ground.

The man with the rifle had a vacant look of someone on a substance. He pointed the gun at the open door.

"That was where he broke in?"

Albert nodded, returning his revolver to its holster.

"Found him with these," Albert said, picking up the bag and offering it, and the hacksaw blade, to the two men.

The Asian man snatched the stuff and threw it in the back of the truck. Then, with a glance at the half-open door of the department store, he handed the flashlight to his companion.

"Check it out."

Dreadlocks disappeared into the store. Albert saw the flashes of light as he moved among the aisles. Presently he emerged with several pairs of trousers slung over the rifle, and shirts and other clothing under both arms.

"They won't miss these," he announced as he threw the merchandise into the back of the jeep.

"Okay. Lock up," the Asian man said.

Dreadlocks walked back to the front of the store, closed the door, and secured it with a pair of handcuffs threaded through the pull bars.

"What about some for him?" Albert said to the long-haired man. Dreadlocks, like his companion, had paid no attention to the youth, who now was trembling on the ground.

The man scratched within his mat of hair as if he was considering the question, then, without any regard for Albert, he barked at the youth:

"Get up, you."

Albert reached downward, and pulling the youth to a standing position made to escort him into the jeep. But Dreadlock's rifle arm came down like a gate.

"Let him go." The order came from behind.

Albert stopped in his stride and turned to find himself confronted by a revolver pointing at his head. Realizing he had no choice, he released the youth who, sensing danger, was already withdrawing by means of backward steps.

"Run, you little animal," the Asian man said. And, as if to show good faith, he stuck the revolver in his belt.

The youth, only half believing his ears, continued to back away slowly. Albert would always remember the white of his eyes, as the youngster searched for a sign of assurance before he broke and ran. He ran with a speed born of terror, streaking away from them along the front of the department store, torn shirt flapping above the wild action of his arms and legs.

Exiles at Home

The first rifle shot missed him and smashed into the glass window of one of the stores at the far end of the complex. The boy swerved to the right, hugging what remained of the night in a desperate attempt to reach the end of the block and escape around the corner of the buildings. Too late he realized that what lay between him and freedom was the light on the fountain. The second shot caught him as he burst out of the shadows. It lifted him off his feet. The wings of the moth opened one last time and drifted towards the spotlight. Then they closed in a heap.

"One less to make trouble," Dreadlocks said.

A JOLLY GOOD TIME

1976

*T*wo men, suspected of being escapees from the General Penitentiary, last night terrorized Shortwood Road area citizens for one hour before the Security Forces got to the scene. The rampage began around 7.30P.M., when a dwelling on Short Wood Lane was entered and a young woman raped...

"Damn bastards," the woman said in the direction of the television. "Should cut off their balls."

"What are balls, mommy?" the daughter enquired, shovelling rice around in her plate.

"Nothing, Mary Ann. If you are not hungry, go to bed, like a good girl."

...Armed with machine guns, the men are reported to have arrived by taxi at a dancehall on Short Wood Crescent and immediately opened fire on the building, killing one man and injuring three other patrons.

"Lance, don't dribble on the dining room floor, darling. Try the tooth brush in the bathroom, like I showed you. Did you hear me?"

"Don't shout, for Christ's sake," the man sitting in the drawing room shouted. "I'm watching the news."

"The dogs must be getting hungry. Have you fed the dogs?'

"Yes, now will you all be quiet, please?"

Addressing the National Youth Brigade this afternoon, the Prime Minister said that nothing would turn back socialism...

"Damn news, gives me indigestion every night. Turn it off, please, David," the woman said, looking at Mary Ann.

"What's that, mommy?"

"I was speaking to your father. For Pete's sake, put the spoon down and go to bed, Mary Ann."

"I have to brush my teeth, mommy." Mary Ann was sucking on the spoon one more time. "Then I have to kiss Daddy."

"All right, all right! Where is Lance? Lance Dawson, put your toothbrush in the glass and climb into bed. Hear mommy, now!"

…Minister of Housing, said the Government would be building two thousand low income houses…

"Can you take over, Maggie. I am tired of the racket."

"Well, sit yourself in the drawing room, dearest husband. Do you want me to bring you some dessert?"

"I don't want any dessert, mommy," Mary Ann said.

"I told you. I am talking to your father. Should cut off their tails, those murderous bastards!"

"Lance has a tail, mommy," Mary Ann confided loudly, jumping off her chair and accidentally toppling it over with a crash on to the mahogany floor.

David walked over to the television, and turned up the sound.

"No dessert, thanks. Can't you all be quiet? I can't hear."

The telephone rang, averting a showdown between the noise in the dining room and the louder one in the drawing room. With Mary Ann hugging one of her legs, Maggie made it across to the telephone table beside the sofa. The caller sounded very excited.

"Hi, Maggie. Surprise, surprise!"

"Mom, is that you? It's my mother, David – the line is very bad. Turn it down, please"

"Guess where we are?" the crackling personage asked. "We are at the Arawak Country Club near Tryall. Flew in this afternoon."

"That is fantastic! What a surprise! David, they are in the

Montego Bay area."

"Oh Gowrd," David said.

"…David there?"

"Yes, mom. Everyone's here. We are so happy you called!"

"How are Mary Ann and the baby?"

"Fine. Mary Ann: say hello to Grandma Sutton. Remember Grandma Sutton, Mary Ann?"

Mary Ann buried her head in Maggie's lap.

"Okay, I'll take her," David said as he separated Mary Ann from her mother and took her half-asleep into her room.

Back in the drawing room, Lance had taken his sister's place in Maggie's lap.

"No go, mom. Mary Ann's gone to bed. When do you arrive in Kingston?"

"Oh Gowrd," David said.

"Dad's in a seniors' tournament that came up quite suddenly. Then we are due to stay a few days over at Stroud Hall Estate. You remember those folks - the Strouds?"

"Yes, of course. Well, vaguely."

"The daughter, Emily, and the Farnam boy are getting married. It's time - she must be twenty six! We came down with our friends, the Thompsons - remember the Canadian gentleman with the patch? Years ago at Stroud Hall? A beautiful setting that house."

Maggie looked away from David who, with head and hand, was begging that she not suggest something. She did. "After that, with us here, of course? Even for a day or two?"

"Instead, Maggie. We were hoping you could come over here and bring the kids. It would be delightful if you could come to Montego Bay. I think Dad would prefer that. You know how he's scared of driving on these roads."

"Drive? But only… Dave! I'm trying to hear mom. Lance is very tired, darling. See to his teeth…."

With a sigh, David turned off the television and, deftly prying Lance out of his wife's lap, disappeared with him into the bathroom.

"What is that?" Maggie said into the phone.

"Have you seen the news?"

"No. Dave has," Maggie replied, crossing gym-slim legs in defence of the carping to come.

"What a terrible thing with that shooting so close to you."

"Yes, but not that close to us - didn't know what had happened until this morning's news."

"It must be getting worse, Maggie. We are both so worried about you!"

"Election time, mom. You know what that's like. Don't worry, for Christ's sake!"

"We do worry. Every day we hear about some dreadful incident. Last week Don Sutherland came up and told us about the Mannings…"

"That was very tragic," Maggie agreed, resigned now to a well-meaning harangue.

"What a wicked thing to do though, eh?"

"Yes, mom. Really bad… David! Are you checking on Mary Ann…? That was Dave in the bedroom, mom. You want to speak to him? He is coming…."

Maggie put her hand on the mouthpiece. "Do you want to say hello?"

"Say hello for me," David whispered, tip-toeing out of the bedroom to sit next to his wife on the sofa, and kissing her ear as a tease.

"He's looking after the kids," Maggie said into the phone. "We'll be very disappointed if we don't see you. It's nearly two years since you left…"

"We hoped you'd come over to this side of the island."

"We would love that," Maggie said. "Trouble is, David's in

the middle of a very important project. Your flying over here would save on expensive telephone calls."

At the other end of the line the exchange ended in laughter.

"It's only play-money, your father says."

"No, mom. It must be part of your hotel bill, and tourists can't pay hotel bills in local currency any more...," Maggie said, smiling to herself.

Now, the crackling sounded very alarmed. "My God! You mean we must pay in real money? That's daylight robbery....Why do you think we gave your address?"

It was Maggie's turn to laugh out loud. "Mom – Don't worry. we'll handle it from here."

"That is what your father thought."

"Well then, telephone calls from a hotel are also costly. Hang up, and I'll phone you right back."

There was a grown, followed by dial tone.

"She's hung up. Stop that, David... and don't ridicule my sweet, irrepressible mother. Pass me the telephone book, darling."

"Sweet, yes of course, but so naive," David said, reaching for the phone book under the coffee table. "Forgotten the number already?"

"I never got the number. They're at Arawak Country Club; so look it up for me."

"One moment," he said as he flipped through the directory pages. "Polo, is it?"

"No, golf."

He held up the book, finger on the number. Maggie dialled and got through to the room. A deep voice came on the line, loud and clear.

"It's Maggie. How are you, daddy?"

"I should be asking you that, My Love. Your mother and I and all the folks in Canada worry about you people down here."

"We're fine, daddy."

"You must be the only ones left!"

"Almost. It's true - lots of our friends are leaving."

"So, when will you follow suit, Maggie?"

"Cannot say."

"You mean you think about it sometimes? David's folks are fine. We keep in touch, though we seldom see them."

Maggie noticed the sound approaching. The noise overhead became deafening. Suddenly, the lawn and the pool area were lit up like the day. On the veranda the dogs started to howl and thrash around on their chains. Lance came stumbling out of his bedroom crying. Instinctively, Maggie dropped the phone and picked him up.

"There, there, little man. You've heard that before," she said, handing the baby to her husband. The roar overhead receded. David was holding Lance close to him in order to muffle the crying.

Maggie retrieved the phone with the caller caught the middle of an exasperation.

"… are you alright?"

"Only a helicopter, daddy."

"Only? I could almost hear it without benefit of the phone. What the heck is going on?"

"They must be patrolling. It's routine these days."

"I asked you whether you ever consider leaving that madness, Maggie?"

"Yes and no, daddy."

"What sort of answer is that?"

"You know how difficult it is. How can we just leave all we have worked for?"

"Jump on the next plane. That's how easy. Look how many have done so?"

"I guess…"

"We have a room for you in Toronto. You both know that.

There's a good kindergarten less than a mile away that would take your Mary Ann tomorrow if you came up.

"What about David? He's got his practice; and I've the clinic. We have all our money tied up here. You know that. Leaving is one thing, but what will we have when we arrive in Canada?"

"Peace of mind, Maggie."

Maggie covered the mouthpiece. "Pour me one, with ginger ale," she said to her husband.

David complied as best he could with Lance on his shoulder.

"Thanks, Hun... Not you Dad...I was asking Dave for something..."

"Peace of mind is very important. Don't you agree?"

"Yes, yes, dad. But we have to weigh peace of mind against drawbacks: like no work. We have two kids. We are well off here. Why throw it all away and risk beginning again - with nothing?"

"So, David would have to go back to the books for a short while..."

"Two years, I think, daddy."

"Well, Mike Simons did it. He's recently been offered a partnership in Hamilton. You should see the mansion they're building."

"I prefer not to see it. Mike is a kid compared to David. Do you expect David to become an apprentice-draftsman all over again? Delivering letters and cow-towing to some stuffed-shirt? It would kill him..."

"Think of the kids, Maggie. Think of them. I can be frank with you about these things. You must do the same with David."

"We've hashed over this stuff many times. Can't we find a more agreeable subject to discuss?"

"I want you tell me you will think about it, Maggie."

"I...believe...Maybe I should ring you back tomorrow."

"Wait Mag. We have lots more to talk about. If you don't want to spend your own money, Owen Stevens can break one of my fixed deposits. Ask him to pay this hotel bill through you."

Maggie would have lost control had David not brought her the whisky.

"Don't you ever think that Jamaica may need the foreign exchange, daddy," she said. She knew full well the suggestion would get his goat.

"Are you joking, girl? Why should we want to spend real dollars here, when we can spend the hard earned Jamaican dollars we had to abandon when we left? Those damned socialists...."

"Anyway, daddy, I told mom we will pay the bill, assuming the hotel has our address on the tab. You can deposit the Canadian dollars in Toronto for us, okay?"

"Yes. I like that alternative, for your sake Maggie. Remember, there are other ways to handle this sort of problem, too."

Maggie was ready to give up on the call. There was nothing she could contribute to the conversation, except remind her father that a few Jamaicans were living high on the hog abroad while island stores were empty. But he wouldn't appreciate that.

"Let us know how much the bill comes to, daddy. And I must go, you hear?"

The querulousness at the other end would not be silenced.

"I hope we agree on the main issue, Maggie. If not Canada, you can apply for a Green Card to the States, just in case."

She removed the phone from her ear, and looked in vain at her husband for assistance. He appeared to be giving all his attention to Lance, rocking him and humming to him, even though he was asleep.

"I can't leave the clinic just like that," she said. "How can I just up and leave? Do you know that last week three children died of advanced malnutrition because of the situation in the back-country?"

"I know, Maggie. I know. But think of your kids too..."

"You left without any guilt-trip from us, daddy. So don't....

"Okay, My Girl. We've discussed this before."

"We feel very indignant when one of Dave's students goes to Toronto, and is spit upon walking down Young Street."

"That may happen in Florida, New Orleans, or anywhere else. Dave's students are mostly black. You are not."

"Surely that's not the point, Daddy. If that happens to black Jamaicans, we don't want any part of it."

"Don't be naive, Maggie. You're living in a country that was once the bedrock of western slavery."

"Yes, we know that."

"Your mother and I don't understand what is holding you there against common sense, against better judgment. And we hate meddling, believe me."

Her father sounded hurt. He always did, when faced with what he regarded as 'irrational' behaviour.

"We know you mean well, daddy, but we have our lives to live."

There was a grunt at the other end of the line.

"Survival is the key, my child. I wish I could get through to David and you. At least we have the freedom to walk on the road in Toronto without being shot at. And every one of us is relieved to have gotten out before Bank of Jamaica closed the doors. Think of that, Maggie. Those damn socialists will soon prevent you from taking out even your furniture!"

"It's not that bad."

"Damned right, it is. You'll be lucky to leave with a suitcase! Remember what happened in Cuba."

"That's US propaganda, daddy. Ever since the bauxite clamp-down by Manley. Destroying our tourism, the US media are. Forgive us if we tough it out a little longer."

"And you forgive us if we disagree with that decision. Every day you stay on the island, you risk being shot, or raped, or something worse..."

"I don't want to hear that, daddy."

"Do you remember the night David and his friend, Anthony, heard someone screaming outside the cinema they were in? When they went to investigate, they found a man with his face hanging open, knife-cut from one ear to the other. Does Dave remember?"

"I am sure he does."

"He and Anthony drove that man to the hospital - bleeding like a pig, we were told."

"Yes, daddy."

"One hundred stitches?"

"Closer to two, actually."

"Where is Anthony today?"

"Georgia." She held out the empty glass. "Neat, this time, please."

David, with Lance still sleeping against him, eased himself out of the sofa and topped it up. She winked at he went to put the child to bed. The obfuscation at the other end continued unabated: Were they not being selfish? Everyone in Toronto was worrying about them being here all alone, defenceless against hooligans. What was the point? How would they live with themselves if Mary Ann were to be molested? It became very difficult for her to contain her frustration.

"Good God, daddy, don't you know how often we have heard all that? Don't you hit us with that sort of blackmail?" She knew immediately, from the stony silence at the other end of the line, that she had overstepped the bounds of civility. Her father was hurt.

But something else was causing her alarm. David, too, had heard the low warning growls of the dogs. He came running out of Lance's room, just as the barking increased with guttural ferocity. Turning off the drawing-room light, and also the outside pool-lights, he reached behind the bookshelf on the far side of the room. By that time the animals were howling, and straining at their leashes.

"Hang on, hang on. The dogs are angry - something outside. Don't go outside, David....Do you hear?"

David hissed at her to be quiet. He had crept up to the window overlooking the lawn and pool area.

"What is happening, Maggie...?" His fear was real. This time it was mutual.

"As I told you, daddy," she said with difficulty, the sight of the object in her husband's hand producing dryness in her throat.

The phone began to crackle. "Are you alright?"

She sat rooted to the sofa. Her imagination was running riot. What would she do if she heard shots, or if *they* should suddenly confront her here, in her drawing room? What if, suddenly, David was dead: shot like John Manning was, just outside his home? She remembered his wife in hospital, with that fixed stare, the hopelessness in her face.

The bedlam had subsided. David was away from the window. Grudgingly, she brought the static to her ear. If only she could bring the conversation to an end.

"A couple of kids on the street," David whispered in her direction. "Maybe they tried to come in." He proceeded to switch on the lights and return the object to its hiding place.

"Good God, Maggie, are you alright?"

"Not to worry. Believe me, daddy," she said at last. "The dogs got excited, that's all. Have a good game tomorrow. We'll call you after dinner." Not waiting for a response, she hung up the phone. Then she downed the whisky so fast her throat erupted. Surrendering to the convulsions, she felt the evening flow slowly down her cheeks.

THE WHOLE TRUTH

1980

A lexandra knew her husband was edgy by his silence. Her job, as she saw it, was to make his life easier in these days of uncertainty. As the Jaguar exited the Commonwealth Club, it was understandable if he was not thinking about his paper.

"Everybody enjoyed it, Bertie," she said in an attempt to placate him.

"Maybe," Bertie Lawrence said.

"Standing ovation, darling."

"The press will have the last laugh."

Yes, Bertie had initiated the whole business of their leaving four months ago, lectured the children about it and arranged the sale of their home. But, for him, reservations had not been far below the surface.

"Well, thank God the paper was not on emigration," she said.

"Forgetting the title? *'The Consequences of Disinvestment and Capital Flight.'* Less damning for me, than emigration?"

It didn't matter that the luncheon was a sell-out and his speech a great success. Today, after months of soul-searching, the fact that Bertie could muster only a comforting side-glance at her as they merged with the traffic, told her he had not achieved closure with what they were about to do.

"Have some faith, darling." Alex was busy shaping the tresses about her ears in defiance of the rain drops appearing on the windshield. She had made the appointment two weeks before; and since then, sometimes noisily, sometimes plaintively, they had wrestled with its life-changing implications. What she knew was difficult for Bertie was his having to maintain the fiction that he was committed to the bank, and of course the well-being of the economy and the country at large.

"Faith, yes. But only when we've flown the coop," Bertie said.

"Guess you've no other choice."

"Except to get the hell out?"

"No. To speak as an economist. You're are not responsible for government policy."

"God forbid."

They drove on in silence. The drizzle was less persistent, but the traffic was slow for most of the way.

"Damn weather," she said.

At the Half Way Tree intersection, even with much horn blowing and swearing, six minutes elapsed while a coconut vender served customers from his mule-cart, in the middle of the road.

Although at the start Bertie had pushed the decision to leave, of late he had been pulling back. Hers had been the job to reassure him that their plans were solid, and that the secrecy and pretences that clouded their lives were worth the effort. Uncertainty about the future, coupled with client responsibilities, had translated into his coming home, on a regular basis at lunchtime, to rest an ulcer.

"The children are exited, Bertie. Jane says she wants to see a snowman walk."

"Would you believe it? The rain has stopped! Maybe the day

has come for us to oblige them."

The limestone building housing the embassy, gleamed in the cool sunlight. Stunted Royal Palms decorated the front gate, and at the end of the driveway, guarding the front entrance, were two Jamaica Constabulary policemen with rifles, standing at attention. Leaving the car park, Alex led the way via a flagstone footpath to the building.

"Hope you brought the envelope," Bertie said.

"As we discussed."

Alex peered into her handbag to make sure. She knew Bertie had reason to be nervous. Every stone was a step towards a questionable future, and away from the one he had planned for himself before they met twelve years ago. She looked back to find he was lagging behind. "Yon Cassius thinks too much," she called over without looking back.

"Right behind you, Pet."

"We'll feel better, when it's all over," she said, stopping until he caught up.

They mounted steps flanked by the two policemen, and entered a darkened room full of what appeared to be disgruntled people, most of them sitting classroom-style in rows of fibreglass chairs, while at the back of the room others stood in lines before windows cut in the glass partition. Many were fanning themselves with whatever was at hand.

"Power cut get we," a woman said as they went by.

Behind the partition the fixed smiles and assured demeanour of two manicured young ladies directing applicants contrasted with the general sourness of the crowd. "No, madam. You will have to bring a letter from the person you will be staying with in Toronto. I am so sorry you had to come all the way from the country." "Sir, these photographs have not been certified, as required by the Regulations. Can you come back when this is done?" "You are on the wrong floor, sir. Canadian residency - third floor."

"We're on the wrong floor," Bertie said.

With an eye on her watch, Alex negotiated their way through the perspiration and cheap perfume, locating the staircase. On the third floor, a stout blonde woman, with a French accent, showed them to a small waiting room where they found a motorcycle policeman in high-boot uniform sitting alone. Alex thought he looked uneasy, before she realized he was there for the same reason they were.

"I hope they will waive the certificate," Alex said, as the power was restored and the merciful air-conditioning came on.

They took the chairs in the corner nearest the air-conditioner.

"Damn fool requirements, all these formalities," Bertie said.

Reminded of the document she was supposed to bring, Alex was frantically hunting around in the purse, only to find something else.

"I told you I couldn't locate that certificate, Bertie. They want the letter too, remember? Here it is."

"The certificate was on my desk in the library, My Sweet."

"I'll bring it down, tomorrow," Alex said, and seeing no reason to be concerned, extracted her compact from the purse. Flipping up the mirror, she proceeded to apply rouge to her upper cheekbones, blending the colour into pale hollows below. "They must recognize who we are, darling," she said through dabs of powder.

"Of course. You are an exceptional first-world wife and mother, and I am a frustrated third-world economist."

"You worry too much," she said, returning the bits and pieces to her purse, before rummaging around in it once more, until she found her cigarette holder and cigarettes. She allowed Bertie to light one for her just as an elderly Chinese couple appeared and took seats near the policeman. He immediately complained about

about the frequency of power-cuts.

"Yea. Not to worry," Bertie said. "Like John and Joyce - turned down in similar circumstances. And they had lots of money out."

"John didn't have a job. And anyway, a lot depends on the interviewer. Remember, Joyce warned us about evasiveness."

"What do we have to hide, My Pet? Look at Dave and Maggie Dawson. They got their papers last year, even though they have no intention of leaving the island just yet, if at all."

"Except that the embassy knew nothing about that."

The French woman appeared at the door and beckoned that they come forward.

"Mr. Hasting will see you now. Room number eight - through the passage."

Mr. Hasting was a fleshy fifty year old, balding prematurely, and wearing a rakish moustache beneath a red nose. He remained in his chair and did not smile or extend a hand when they entered his spacious office. Instead he motioned them to be seated in front of his desk, on which was a pink note pad and a file. But what was actionable was the large wooden paperweight. Embellished on it were the words, *Thank you for not smoking*.

"Have you brought the documents?" Hasting asked, appearing not to notice that Alex had to rise from her chair in order to reach the ashtray beside the desk.

She then handed him the letter, which he spread on the desk in front of him but did not read.

"So you want to migrate with your family to Canada?"

"Yes, as soon as possible," Bertie said.

From his file Hasting pulled their application and studied it for a moment.

"You have three children?"

"Michael fifteen and Sarah twelve...." Alex began.

"Yes, I see. Why do you want to live in Winnipeg?"

"We..." Alex began again.

Hasting ignored her.

"Have you ever been to Winnipeg, Mr. Lawrence?"

"Not really."

Without warning their interviewer's tone became hostile.

"Either you have or you haven't."

"Well, I have been to Canada; not yet to Winnipeg."

Using the back of his thumbs in succession Hasting smoothed the sides of his moustache.

"You applied specifically for Winnipeg, Mr. Lawrence."

Feeling very uncomfortable, Alex avoided eye-contact with the man on the other side of the desk. Instead, she looked down at her hands. These interviews could be intimidating, she had heard. Yet details of what one could expect were vague - almost as if the so called "meeting before the Commissioner" was an embarrassment that applicants preferred not to reveal to others.

"Well, I don't know. I mean..."

"You don't know?" Hasting put his elbows on the desk. "This interview has hardly begun and already I feel you're wasting my time, Mr. Lawrence. I am extremely busy..." Extending his arms as if he was lost for words, he rose from his chair and moved towards the door.

Instinctively, Alex jumped up and tried to cut him off.

"My husband meant..."

"Please bear with us," Bertie said, half rising from his chair.

Seeing the anguish on her husband's face, Alex retraced her steps and stood beside him. Hasting had almost reached the door before he relented.

"Please remain seated," he said, once he was. "Now, can we restart this interview?"

"Of course, and thank you for your patience," Bertie said. "You see, I was about to say...."

"Never mind that. Tell me why you want to leave Jamaica."

Afraid her husband was at the end of his patience and might throw the whole interview, Alex reached over and took hold of his arm in an attempt to calm him down. Hasting may consider him crushed and vulnerable, but she knew there was a limit beyond which Bertie would react in unpredictable ways.

"It is not my intention to run down this country," Bertie said.

"Please, Mr. Lawrence, that's irrelevant. I did not ask you to do that."

Before they filed their application, they had thrashed out the issues surrounding their departure. They even convinced themselves they had found satisfactory answers. Now, Alex saw that Bertie was struggling to put them into words.

"I just delivered a paper in praise of this country...." he was looking at her for support. "However, these days we find ourselves alone. Do you understand that, Mr. Hasting? Friends and family have left. We've begun to look upon ourselves as strangers here, part of an out-of-place minority, if you see what I mean."

For Alex, the sinking feeling had returned. What was obvious was Hasting's apparent intention to ask questions that led only to other questions.

"That's hardly an answer," Hasting said, looking only at Bertie. "You've become strangers in your country, so you want to fly to mine where you will be even more estranged! You don't want to be in a minority here, but wish to be a part of a small group of Jamaicans, if you are lucky, far away in Canada."

"We know our reasons seem funny to you," Alex interjected, trying to reduce the pressure on her husband.

Hasting was not smiling as he turned to her for the first time.

"Funny is it, Mrs. Lawrence? I would call it ridiculous."

Alex was determined to avoid Hasting's indifferent stare. "If you must know the details, my family recently moved from

Toronto to Winnipeg, and my brother has opened a business there. So we decided to join them."

"How old are you, Mrs. Lawrence?"

She hesitated, reaching for a cigarette only to replace it in the pack when she remembered the sign on the desk.

"Forty," she said, completely deflated.

"And you expect me to believe that the main reason you want to leave this country is that you need mother and father?"

"Of course not!" She felt that Hasting's impertinence had reached a new high. "We thought it would be best for our children, who are still in school, to grow up near their grandparents."

"Have you been to Winnipeg, Mrs. Lawrence?"

"No, but we have visited the...."

"I didn't ask you that. How can you know what it will be like living in Winnipeg, when neither of you has taken the trouble to go there?"

Alex could see difficulties ahead. Before she could reply, Hasting, who had been looking through the papers, scowled at Bertie.

"I don't see a school leaving certificate for you, Mr. Lawrence. Did you not know we required it for this interview?"

"Yes, I..."

"Where is it?"

"I have had some difficulty getting it from my old school."

"Come, come. When we set this interview date, you undertook to provide us with all the documentation supporting your application, did you not? You have chosen to treat this matter lightly?"

"I am an economist out of LSE. Certainly...."

"That's not the question, sir."

Again Alex could see anger in her husband's face. He was a naughty kid lost for excuses and awaiting punishment. Whatever apprehensions she may have had about this meeting, cold, calculated intimidation was not one of them.

"I am mortified," Bertie said, bitter sarcasm evident in his tone of voice.

"What will you do in Winnipeg, Mr. Lawrence?" Again, the direct question, the menacing tone that gave no quarter.

They had prepared for this question as probably the most important of the interview, since none of their friends had been granted permanent residence without a "job offer". Alex knew that Bertie had worked it out, so that he could not possibly fail on this account. Yet she saw him hesitate, as if he was not sure of his answer.

"I've been offered a job by my brother-in-law."

Hasting seemed unimpressed. Looking at the papers before him, he murmured something, smoothing his moustache as he made a note on the pink pad. Alex realized that he smoothed his moustache, whenever he was about to pounce.

"I see that," Hasting said. "Is this matter the subject of a letter from your brother-in-law?"

"Yes. I enclosed a copy with my application."

"And where is the acknowledgement from the authorities in Winnipeg?"

"On its way, I'm told," Bertie said hastily, and then tried to retract the lie, seeing that the letter was on his desk at home. "At least, that is what I understand…"

"What business is your relative in, Mr. Lawrence?"

"Hardware."

Bertie seemed to be more relaxed, but Alex had a bad feeling this would not last.

"What does he deal in, mainly, that is?"

"Lumber, logs, I think."

"You think?"

"Yes… I…"

Hasting was not impressed. "What size business? How many people does the business employ? What's the turnover?"

"It's not a large operation. I am not sure of the turnover ..."

Again her husband was on the defensive. Their story was collapsing under the weight of silly questions neither of them had foreseen. If only she had found that damned letter.

"Your present salary according to this application is forty thousand dollars. Do you mean to tell me a small business can afford to pay you that?"

"Probably."

"Probably? You have agreed to go into business, but you are not sure what type of business it is, or even whether it can afford to pay you?"

"I trust him."

Alex could not contain herself.

"Are you implying my husband is lying? Don't you have my brother's letter before you?"

Hasting was unmoved. Ignoring her and her question he continued to address Bertie.

"It is quite easy to get a letter from a close relative, Mr. Lawrence. In your case, you haven't taken the trouble to do a little homework to back up your story. It may interest you to know that, in my country, hardware merchants do not usually handle logs."

"I apologize."

"And I must tell you that this interview is not going well."

"What do you want me to say?"

"I want the truth, Mr. Lawrence."

"I told you I was going to work with my brother-in-law."

"Do you know that Winnipeg has one of the highest unemployment rates in Canada, Mr. Lawrence?"

"Maybe. Is it important?"

"Do you think I can allow folks to enter without jobs, and add to the number on welfare?"

Furious, Alex was shaking her fist at Hasting before she realized what she was doing. "Do we look like that sort?"

Again, Hasting ignored her. "Sir, you look like someone who has come in here with a trumped up job offer from a relative."

Alex saw their hopes slipping away. The worst had happened. They were on their knees against a wall, with no wiggle-room. Could it be that Bertie was on the wrong side of the desk? He was accustomed to ask, not answer questions. Or could it be he was unschooled in bluffing his way out of tight corners? An impasse surely. Yet, with it had come a certain resignation. For she noticed that he had leaned back in his chair for the first time in many minutes. Even though he had lost the catch-me-if-you-can game he seemed surprisingly relaxed.

"I don't have to work in my brother-in law's business, do I? You asked me if I had a job and I told you he had offered me one…. I didn't say I was definitely going to work with him, or for him."

"Do I understand it correctly that, contrary to previous assertions in this matter, you will not be employed in his store?"

"I might, and I might not be. There are other positions that I am investigating."

"I see."

Hasting's nose seemed redder than before as he thumbed through his file. Finally, he extracted a document on which he wrote something before he creased it down the middle with his thumb.

"Many of you well-off folks make applications, and think that you have a right to live in my country and enjoy all the benefits it provides. Do you believe you have such a right, Mr. Lawrence?"

Bertie Lawrence shrugged. Alex attempted to say something but their inquisitor put his hand up to stop her.

"In Canada there are public benefits such as unemployment insurance, welfare, universal health care, government pensions - apart from the lowest crime rate in the western hemisphere. These advantages are afforded to us by our laws, and by taxpayers, whose contributions to the public purse I must consider."

"We appreciate all that," Bertie said.

For the first time Hasting smiled, and caught off guard, Bertie followed suit. But then their inquisitor's face clouded again as he scrutinized the file.

"I see that you have a Mr. Lawrence, Sr., as your sponsor?"

"Yes."

"And what would his Canadian income, or his assets, amount to?"

"I don't know. My father's retired," Bertie said.

Hasting looked at the ceiling, shaking his head in apparent disbelief.

"So, Mr. Lawrence, I can ask only that you appreciate the difficulty I have. Stand in my shoes. Would you admit to this island, as permanent residents, a family of five wherein neither parent had a credible job offer or visible means of support; and more than that, in circumstances where their only sponsor could not support them in a crisis?"

Alex saw her husband shift in his chair before what was certain to be an explosion of indignation. Without doubt, the interview was at an end. She was signalling to him that they should leave, when she noticed he was suppressing laughter with a hand over his mouth.

"We fall into that category, do we, Mr. Hasting?"

Hunched forward in his chair, Hasting put his pen on the desk with exaggerated finality.

"There are three kinds of applicants that are successful for Canadian residency, Mr. Lawrence: Those in compliance with the age, health, and other demographics that Canada lays down, those with skills Canada wants, and a few that bring lots of money into the country. Then there are the non-starters: The ones who see Canada only as a country socially safe and secure. They "half-emigrate," with no intention of taking up residence, unless they are forced to do so. Where do you think you rank?"

"Our application is on your desk, Hasting," Bertie said, for the first time dropping the mister.

"I don't know if it's enough, Mr. Lawrence," Hasting said, almost resignedly. "My job is not only to review applications, but also, as I said before, to get to the truth."

"We understand that," Alex said.

Hasting was pouring over the documents, as if for the first time.

"There is no mention here about your bringing money with you to Canada."

Alex was really confused. Where was this interview going? A short time ago it was coming to an ignominious end. Suddenly, Hasting was again on the attack.

"We missed the boat on that matter," she said.

"How so?" Hasting seemed genuinely interested.

"Everyone knows Jamaicans cannot take money out of the country," Bertie said.

"Ah, yes," Hasting said, pushing away the file.

Alex noticed he was back to fingering his moustache. She took the offensive. "Presumably, you would be happier if we got our money out, anyway."

"You misunderstand me, madam," Hasting said, now with elbows again on the desk. "I was referring to the fact that most wealthy Jamaicans that come through this office have much of their capital outside - before they apply!"

"We're no angels. Yet, we have very little money out," Bertie said.

"Without capital you are a potential liability. Are you

comfortable with that?"

"With reservations," Bertie said.

"Please explain."

"My job, maybe."

"Meaning?"

When Bertie seemed to hesitate, Alex felt she should answer for him. "My husband must abide by the rules he imposes on his clients...."

Bertie was having none of it. Visibly upset and out of his chair, he reached for her hand, dropping all formalities.

"My good man, I've had about enough of this. If our capital is the bottom line, we hereby withdraw our applications. Does that make it easier for you?"

Hasting seemed genuinely apologetic as he motioned with open hands that they remain seated. Somehow, he had become a tired old man with a red nose, at the end of a trying day, straining against the urge to embroil himself in an argument he may not win. After a moment of reflection he said, "Fortunately, Canada will survive with or without it, Mr. Lawrence."

Alex knew their fate was sealed. This was an issue Bertie had been grappling with for several weeks leading up to this afternoon's luncheon. Now he was wound up, and angry at his adversary across the desk.

"You said that you wanted the whole truth, Hasting. Well, you can write it down that your country is the major beneficiary in its dealings with this impoverished country. Our bauxite has enriched western British Columbia for decades, indeed has employed many more North Americans than Jamaicans. In addition, the static extraction prices you enjoyed for twenty years resulted in greater and greater trade deficits for us, in light of the escalating cost of aluminium products imported...."

"I don't have to listen to this, Mr. Lawrence."

Alex noticed the hardening in Hasting's approach that

promised no hope for the meeting. And then, sensing the real reason for her husband's shortness of tone, she could almost forgive his forfeiting their chances. He was not unhappy about the turn of events because, deep down, he wanted a refusal. It played into his reluctance to leave the island in the first place. Having eaten humble-pie before this man for his family's sake, he could return to the life he loved, in the country he loved, without regrets.

"Please forgive my husband's bluntness, Mr Hasting. It's been more than we expected."

"I understand, madam."

"I don't believe you do, Hasting," Bertie said, again dropping the mister. "I sit on the boards of three crown corporations and am an advisor to the government. Yet, I cannot buy a bank draft in Canadian or US currency. If I have not visited Winnipeg it is partly because I cannot afford to do so. It is that simple. Canadians can visit their bank and withdraw their money in whatever currency they want. In Jamaica, this is not possible. Can you understand that?"

"Maybe, Mr. Lawrence. We could say it underlines the fact that we sit on opposite sides of this desk."

For the first time it became obvious to Alex that their interrogator was unsure of himself. He was supposed to be the one asking the questions, but suddenly he was the one being questioned. And Bertie had just begun to open up.

"There is a minority of Jamaicans born half in, and half out, of this country," he said. "That's the unfortunate truth. Even when they are half in, their capital is half out. They now consider themselves as mid-Atlantic, if you please. For them, Independence was a disaster. In 1962 some went as far as the Home Office in London to complain that their British passports were taken *without their permission* - replaced by Jamaican ones, if you please - the worst kind of deracination, if you get my drift."

All of a sudden Hasting was listening, with occasional nods indicating a modicum of interest. "At least many of them are still here, Mr. Lawrence. You won't even be half in and half out, will you?"

"I don't believe we have a choice, looking ahead," Alex said, before her husband could reply. She sensed that the irony in Hasting's response was almost placatory.

Bertie was less so. "If Canada turns us down, we will go to England where I was educated, at great cost to this island, I might add. I happen to be one of those valuable "resources" that rich countries extract from poor countries - free, gratis, and for nothing."

Hasting had abandoned the aggressive posture of leaning forward when speaking. Now, he was sitting lower in his chair than before, apparently looking for the right words to use.

"I believe you are both wrong about Canada, Mr. and Mrs. Lawrence," he said, gathering up his papers. "Maybe, one day you will remember I said that."

For Alex the interview was over; except that Hasting was sitting quietly in his chair, as if he was sending them the message that he was not through.

"We did not mean to offend...." she said.

Hasting chuckled, plainly dismissing the need for her remark.

"I too, apologize," he said in his new conciliatory tone. "I believe you both understand that we cannot allow Canada to be used merely as an insurance policy for some applicants, thus reducing the places available for others. Hence the hard line by my Department in these interviews. We must try to get at the truth, by whatever means available."

"Makes sense," Bertie said as he rose to take the hand offered to them across the desk.

"I have another appointment waiting," Hasting said, after shaking their hands in turn. "So I must thank you for coming in.

Your papers will be in the mail. And, before I forget it...
Especially with three children in the family, don't forget to apply
for Canada Health Insurance, as soon as possible after you take
up residence in Manitoba."

AFTERNOON OF HAPPINESS

1995

I was not always seventy seven, lonely, and overweight. Once, decades ago, I was a struggling student of journalism in Toronto, that is, until late 1941 when, caught up in the patriotic spirit of the time, I trained as a navigator for the Royal Air Force, ending up early in 1943 with its nascent Canadian Wing. After losing an eye to shrapnel over Germany I retreated to journalism, mostly on secondment to the Ministry of Information in London, England.

I mention these unimportant events only because they led to my meeting Robert Stroud, and, equally important, his future wife Miriam, who recently departed this world. She had lived much of her long and turbulent life in Jamaica, where, not only was she heir to the Stroud business empire, she was pivotal in its expansion over the years, partnered in latter times by daughter, Emily, and Martin Farnam, Emily's husband. After Miriam's death, the Farnams moved much of their fortune to Toronto, where, with their two teenage boys, they took up residence in Rosedale - almost next door to my home. That was when the pressure on me began in earnest.

Emily was born in England after World War II and spent her early childhood in London, before her parents took her to Jamaica in the 1950s. That was all she had been told, which was little more than she remembered anyway, seeing she was seven when the family left England. The war years and their aftermath remained a tantalizing mystery her parents refused to discuss, except in evasive generalities. So, this was not the first time she had come to Toronto insisting, unsuccessfully in the past, that I put a shine on various nuggets of information she had kept safe in a memory box.

Now, in her forties, Emily Farnam was at the top of her powers as a strong-willed, disarmingly beautiful woman who knew how to get what she wanted. I had nightmares of her rummaging through my books and papers, creeping about in my attic, and camping on my front lawn until I revealed what I knew about the *British phase* of her illusive childhood. It all came down to my providing a written account of that period so that, if she chose she could put it aside until a later date if that was necessary to protect her children from some unsavoury truth - much the same as she had been protected in her time.

Of course, she knew very well that the short-cuts to an aging widower's heart were flattery, frequent visits, and the empty promises of legs and cleavage. I don't deny they were effective. Almost as enticing, were her concessions: I could take whatever liberties I chose in telling the story, and should overlook nothing of which I had even an inkling. Little did she know that many years before she came to live in Toronto I began to write a novel inspired by the same *true story* she was eliciting from me. I abandoned the project because of the pain it likely would have caused eccentric, misunderstood Miriam.

Not only was Miriam a person who kept important things from her daughter, she was twice divorced and resigned to what she called a life of "enduring one marital conflict at a time". After losing all the battles she ended up spending her last years as a demented recluse: burning incense to the Sacred Heart in reparation for sins remembered but not necessarily committed. Needless to say her secrets remained intact. What she should have done years ago I can only attempt to do now. I hope I will be forgiven for relating the story in disparate pieces, necessarily nuanced by the uncertainties that time leaves us, beginning if I may with the least controversial ones.

Sergeant Robert Stroud joined RAF Elsham Wolds as a bomb-aimer midway through 1943, and in August of that year managed a transfer, much as I had, to the Canadian side of the war. Welcoming him to our crew when he arrived at the Blue Nose mess hall, I was the first person to offer him a cup of tea. His dry humour attracted me from the beginning. "The weather is less blimey over here," he said without a trace of rancour.

Over-here was the Tholthorpe Base, the home of the newly constituted Royal Canadian Air Force, which was then about to commence sorties into Germany and Italy. Over-here was the green fields of Yorkshire, blessed with a view of the Hambleton Hills and their 300' cut-out of the *White Horse of Kilburn*, which in retrospect was so fateful for Robert.

A stoop short of six foot two inches tall, wiry and athletic, he had a face prematurely lined by the sun and a personality that was volatile and solitary all at once - a mountainous terrain full of rocky slopes and inaccessible valleys. An only child and heir to large land holdings in Jamaica's interior as well as resort properties on the iconic north coast, he had grown up among the cool hills and plains of Trelawney in a family that went back to the 1860s. From old English stock, his father was a patriarchal type, accustomed to having his way in business matters and otherwise enjoying what the locals referred to as "paramourial" privileges. His doting mother was a Spanish lady from Barcelona, a reluctant islander, and a resentful wife whose self-sacrifice was rewarded by having her only son packed off to Oxford after high-school.

Robert resented that dismissal and, as it turned out, after one year at Balliol was sent down for conduct unbecoming. The story was that he struck a student who allegedly assaulted him, prompting friends to suspect that his cultural conservatism had run up against the dandyism common at Oxbridge before the war. His university days cut short, he returned to Jamaica, only to find his parents embroiled in messy divorce proceedings. Having finally given up on her marriage, his mother, then in her early forties, had fallen for an American banker whom she was seeking to marry if she could get an annulment of her marriage.

In an era when civil divorces were often contested in open court, her case was a particularly traumatic public process, seeing it involved a prominent Catholic wife and mother, and now a foreign "co-respondent". When the annulment was refused she felt she had no choice but to leave the island and throw herself on the mercies of Manhattan.

Unable to cope with these bumps and bruises, Robert sought refuge in another conflict, one which he was to discover few young men survived intact. His aloof disposition was resented by higher-ups who expected a herd mentality among recruits from the colonies. But never did I know him to be the least resentful of this – or to feel out of his depth in dealing with authority.

Yet, I soon learned he was shy, humble, and not above self-deprecating revelations that spoke to inexperience, if not immaturity. Especially as regards English women, his days as a student of the Classics had been aborted before he had the chance to plumb those depths.

The dandelions had all but captured Tholthorpe base that day in early summer, when three of us were taking the sun on the grass outside the mess. Colin, our rear gunner, a freckle-faced fellow from South Wales, known to consider himself a ladies' man, had recounted a story of dubious conquest, when Robert offered his opinion.

"English girls are pretty, but not much spark."

For Colin, this amounted to a personal attack. "How many

lasses 'ave you known, then?"

"Too few to mention, I must admit," Robert said.

"So, apologise, man."

Though visibly uncomfortable, Robert did not back down.

"When you prove me wrong."

"Preposterous, man. How can anyone?"

"You probably know the facts. Mine is an opinion," Robert began in his quiet way, looking intently at Colin. "Come to think of it, being preposterous is a common failing of mine. Before I shipped out of Jamaica I was told all English girls had big ankles. I went to Oxford believing that to be true. Indeed, I refused to look at the women until an Irish friend took me on a prove-it mission to the big city during the Christmas break. He insisted we stand on Piccadilly at store-closing time, and had me promise to point out all the office girls I saw with big ankles. I lost the bet, of course."

"I like that story, brother," Colin said. He would become one of the few men with whom Robert found common ground at Tholthorpe and Croft. That is, until November fourth of that first year, when a 30mm cannon mangled the Welshman in his gun-turret. A month before that I was side-lined out of action, with a patch over my right eye.

I never lost touch with Robert, the patriot who lost faith in the ends pursued by Bomber Command. In March of 1944 having become one of the minor celebrities for surviving thirty missions over enemy targets, he was eligible for extended-leave. Instead, he opted for a desk job at HQ and never returned to active duty. His conflicted personality led to his suffering mental breakdowns that in today's world would be recognized as worthy of a clinical name and drugs to match. Back then, what ailed him was a condition masked by one's inner strength, unnoticed by superiors, and tolerated by everyone else.

For reasons unknown, once the war finally was over, the change in Robert's outlook was nothing less than volcanic. His bi-polar issues still smouldered in the back room, but the stone had been removed from the front door so that he even seemed to stand taller than he had done before. Supported for the most part by money from his father, he rented a flat in Richmond, walking distance from a second hand bookstore where he had taken the job of assistant manager.

In sum, his about-face was all about women. Female conquests became for him the new war, waged valiantly but understood even less than the old one. In those heady times of wild parties leading up to, and following the end of the European conflict, love, or the sex that passed for it, was easy to find in London. Robert's frenetic activities were confined to the latter, except that this existentialist spree was short-lived. For he had jumped into a pond that was more than ankle-deep.

In the spring of 1945, at a rowing party on the Thames, he met Miriam. A vivacious, some would say unstable, thirty two year old, she was some years older. Part Jewish part English on her mother's side, she never knew her Scottish father, a coalminer who had died on the Somme. Having served as a Registered Nurse in London and Rome she was a hardened woman, given to cynicism and apparently oblivious to the old morality that sought to keep them in check.

For her, sex was just a word attached to favours granted sad young men returning from the war, attachments that masked a darker side of a brittle personality. Accomplished at casting for men with bra-less come-ons, she had in her arsenal the promise of an elusive neck, revealed in all its glory whenever she threw her head back in laughter.

On his part, Robert was a questionable catch. He mirrored Miriam's maladjustments and their tumultuous relationship often meant mutual hostility, even in public. But that came later. For eleven months they shared a flat in Richmond, on the river. Robert would boast that their affair was a forest fire only a flood could extinguish. A flood it was.

Years later they again lived together by the Thames. Emily had come along and they did their best to weather their many storms. For they were not happy. Indeed it was Emily who kept them together, and in whose interest they married in 1956 before departing England. Miriam was determined to make a fresh start and convinced Robert they also owed it to the child to do so.

With hope for the future, they booked a suite on a Banana Boat bound for Jamaica, where they lived together in great style until Emily was thirteen years old. For it was in the summer of 1962, at a polo tournament at Stroud Hall, that Robert, 41, was thrown from his recently acquired Albino, and killed.

But, I have jumped years ahead. One of the curious things about relationships of the bedroom, is how quickly they can fall out of bed. Within six months of their getting together, Robert and Miriam's stormy affair was already going sideways. Inexperienced as he was at the time, he failed to see the contradictions that lay below the surface of her capricious personality.

If truth be told, I don't believe he ever did see them. All he knew was that something was bothering her, something she was reluctant to discuss with him and he was happy to avoid. One morning early in August 1945, they were in Petersham Meadows feeding mallards by the water when she confronted him with what he thought afterwards was an ultimatum.

"Quite soon, you will be looking for a younger woman."

"Don't say that, Miriam. You're the restless one, not me."

He tossed another handful of corn among the ripples at the edge of the water, where a mother and four teenage ducklings were waiting patiently.

"See. They are a family," Miriam said, as the birds scurried to collect.

"Not this time, can't you see?"

"What do you mean?"

"Only a mother-duck. No father-figure in sight."

"Bloody chauvinist, you are."

"Why so?"

"Children are what count, Robert."

"You want to spoil a good thing?"

Miriam laughed in the way only she knew how. "Of course not. Why so serious?"

"But you are talking about us?"

"Even mother ducks know what I meant, Robert."

"So, don't deny it. This is about us."

"And what if it were?"

"Why has it not come up before?"

"Because I'm a conniving bitch, Robert."

"Slow down, Miriam. I need time...."

Her face darkened and she seemed to recoil from him.

"Unfortunately, My Love, that's something I don't have to give."

By the end of 1945 he was at a loss to understand what had gone wrong between them. The forest fire had gone out, flood or no flood.

He admitted as much to himself on a wet evening in February 1946. Miriam had a colleague from the hospital, with whom she had gone to the movies on occasion, but whom Robert had never met. On that soggy occasion the two women were to have rendezvoused at the theatre, except that because of a mistake this friend came by to collect Miriam at their flat.

"Miriam left to meet you an hour ago," he said, almost out of breath as he tried not to stare at the most heart-stopping woman he had ever seen. There was an ethereal glow about her that begged him to reach out and touch her, if only to be sure that she was real. "She should be back soon. Do come in out of the rain."

Thus did Robert Stroud welcome Lena Pozner into his life. As she stood by the fire, he knew she was the one for him, even if he could not explain why. Was it founded on pure magnetism, or was it more visceral - like delicate hands with those long, pale fingers? Maybe he was seeing only trivia, like the large earrings hiding among, and blending with, thick strands of gold.

"Do you play the piano, Lena?"

"A little. How did you guess?"

"You look the artistic type."

"Is that how nurses look to you?"

"Tell me more, while I get us some tea."

She had worked under Miriam as a trainee. Polish on her father's side, German on her mother's, she was nearly thirteen when, because of mounting tension between the two countries in 1938, she was spirited out of Poland to a private boarding school in London. Less than a year later, she was technically an orphan having lost, first her mother during the bombing of their home-town of Wielun on the first day of Hitler's invasion of western Poland, and, soon afterwards, her father, who was presumed imprisoned if not killed by the Russians when they annexed the Brest Region of the country.

"So what happened to you?"

"Without funding I ended up a ward of the British Government. Transferred to Solihull, I was. There, a Catholic orphanage/boarding school called Waverley, run by one Adelaide Porter, became my home. A great lady she was beloved by all the girls. After four years, just short of eighteen, I left to commence training at St. Bartholomew Hospital, where I met Miriam. And that's enough about me."

Robert said very little that evening, satisfied to be able to gaze unabashed at Lena, flushed with emotion as she recounted her story. There she stood, illuminated by the fire, not completely comfortable, the curved promise in her fine-boned frame daring him to accept that something was happening between them.

He was discovering that the need to possess another person can be uncontrollable, that preordained rules of engagement are no match for human desire. In the weeks that followed, it seemed Miriam saw only what she wanted to see, until Robert left her with hardly a goodbye.

In Lena he had found the fulfilment and purpose for which he had prayed his whole life, and for which he was willing to forsake all others. There was no other way except to do it by the book. Late one evening in April they were almost at the end of a stroll across London Bridge when he summoned up the courage to pose the question.

"I don't ask that we live together, Lena. Marry me. Right now, tonight."

She stopped and looked at him, her troubled frown a veil across her face. "I can't. I'm, I'm....Bobby, is it possible to love someone dearly, but not know whether you're ready for....?"

He held her - questioning, protesting, begging. To no avail. She broke free and ran across the remaining span, leaving him frozen to the ground. Before he could take serious chase she had hopped on a bus and disappeared.

For the first time in his life Robert had let down his guard without reservation, exposing feelings he did not know he possessed, only to be rebuffed. Nothing had prepared him for this or the fact that, having burned the bridge behind him, now he also had burned the one in front.

The next six weeks, during which Lena refused to see him,

were like an eternity. Then, without any forewarning she appeared at his door one evening and refused to come inside before he was onside regarding her proposition.

"I've reconsidered what you asked, Robert," she said, holding the door open as if nervous that he would close it in her face. "If you still want me, I want you. Can't we can live together - even if I cannot promise marriage."

"You know I love only you, Lena."

Letting go of the door she stepped inside the room and collapsed into his arms. "Is that a yes, Bobby."

During 1946 I made several trips to London for my Toronto newspaper, during which I visited with my friend and his picture-book partner. Robert had changed - grown up even. For the first time in his life he had found real contentment. The moody, almost sullen person had become almost mercurial. In May, or thereabouts, we were rowing on the Serpentine when he broke the news that Lena was pregnant. I did not hear the full story of that tragedy until much later.

1947 was not a good year. By the early fall of 1948 the relationship was on life support, and Robert was asking himself questions uncannily similar to the ones for which he had found no answers three years earlier: What makes parting inevitable rather than contingent? Is the point of no return reached when seen by both partners simultaneously, or does one of them usually see it before the other? Can civility alone sustain a relationship? Does abstinence increase, or decrease desire? For him these conundrums were dead weights around his neck during the Indian summer of that year.

He had made up his mind. The next question was when. One answer came in the form of a message. Miss Porter was ailing, and Lena insisted they visit the old lady together. Here was something he could do for her before telling her of his decision. With the proviso that he would not discuss the war, he agreed to accompany Lena to Solihull. In the interim, the bizarre result of the sad news was that both their spirits rose.

As the day approached Lena came alive. The evening before they left London she stayed up late in order to make snacks for the train journey and pack stuff for an over-night in Solihull. The next morning there she was at Paddington Station - an unusual blush in her cheeks and sparkle in her eyes, outfitted in blue-jeans and matching shoulder-bag - waiting it seemed not so much for a train but for some secret delight. When ruminating about his life Robert would return to that day he finally accepted that happiness is a delusion born of hope.

Sharp at 9.19AM the platform of the Western Region, London to Birmingham, Express was enveloped in steam as the King Class behemoth grunted, stirred, and as if in distress, rolled out of the station. Three hours later they were alighting in the medieval borough town of Lena's youth.

Robert was prepared for emotions running high, especially after Lena's insistence that they take a "sentimental walk" through a park bordering Waverley. From where the bus stopped it did not look much like a park. Across the entrance was a rusty cattle-crossing, flanked by skeletal saplings bereft of their roundish, half-trodden, yellow leaves that lay on the foot-path.

"Let's get off this pathway," Lena said, tugging at his coat. "We can cross the field. It's much nicer."

Once they were in the open they felt the wind and the grass was noticeably wet.

"We used to have picnics on a clearing by the river," she said.

Already, the emotion he must try to counter. "River?"

She pointed in the distance. "Not yet. Beyond the oak trees, over there. See, the breeze is undressing them."

"Love it. Just love it. Is that what they are? Anyway, it can't be the same river, dearest."

"Are you having me on, Bobby?"

"Course not. You said it all."

The ground rose. They were traversing a carpet of red and brown that crunched under-foot. Seeing the tears, he put his arm around her waist, pulling her closer.

"It's the smell," she said, holding her nose. "I forgot about the smell."

"Happens at this time every year."

"I don't like it - that sickly-sweet odour."

"Autumn rot. New earth forming," he said, opening his arms and breathing in the fetid air.

"New life eludes us, Robert."

Suddenly her thighs blended with his as they walked. Then almost as quickly they were gone.

"Your teeth are chattering, Lena."

"Full moon tonight. I hate the cold."

"I remember when you didn't."

"Whatever do you mean?"

"I mean, that first evening - when you appeared on my balcony. Hardly a stitch on, as I recall."

"You must have been imagining things,"

"And then some."

Stumbling over words she tried to say something, then stopped. Finally, they tumbled out. "Lust at last light. That's it, Bobby. A poetic description of the evening."

"Don't, Lena. You know better than that."

She was already walking on.

"Passion is destructive without the other thing, Bobby"

"Really? Do we have either?"

"Yes, I know. I'm trying, Bobby."

"How much more of this, Lena. How much more?"

"Soon. I want….You're leaving me soon, aren't you?"

"You know I won't, Lena." He reached for her hand to excuse the lie. A desperate need made him stop. Taking hold of her, he drew her close only to feel her stiffen ever so slightly, yet enough that their fleeting intimacy ended almost before it began.

"The path, at last," she said, changing the subject. "See? I remembered - except that the poplars are a forest now."

"Forest primeval."

"Okay. I deserve to be made fun of. I suppose the property will be sold when she dies."

"Stop it, Lena."

"Well that's true, isn't it?"

"Who said she's dying?"

"All around us is death."

"Let's not get all morbid again."

She squeezed his hand. "I hardly recognize this place."

He knew she was upset when she let go.

"Easy now, My Lady. We've lots of time."

"Maybe we should go back."

"Go back? Are you bonkers?"

"I'm afraid, Bobby. Miss Porter won't understand us." And brushing a golden strand from her face, she reached up with a flourish and tweaked his ear. "She doesn't know we're living in sin."

"Careful - it would be two-faced to say we were!"

"I was only trying to be nice."

"Anyway, you decided it. Forget I asked for your hand?"

"Corny idea."

"Yes. But I must confess I fell for your exquisite hands before I fell for you. Is it possible to fall in love with a woman's hands?"

"For Christ's sake, shut up. You didn't want to bring me."

"Of course I wanted to, damn it."

"I do want to see her again. Look, the top of the house!"

In the distance beyond a wooden bridge, Georgian chimneys

loomed above the trees.

"At least we won't have to search for it," he said.

Beaming with anticipation she was ahead of him, waltzing with the shoulder-bag. "This reminds me of walks in the park back home. Mama used to take me to see the swans."

"Haven't heard you speak of her for many a month."

"She would have been so happy you brought me here today."

"I'm glad."

"What about yours, Bobby? She's yours to have. Mine is not."

"The choice was hers. I'm out of it - both of them."

"Not quite. Your father sends…"

"Conscience money. The least he can do. Let's not get into it."

"I'm not angry with you, Bobby."

"Neither am I with you."

"But you feel 'out of it' with me too – just as…"

"Stop it, Lena."

"Tell me you still care, even a little."

"Very much," he said, without feeling. From her blank stare he knew she had not heard.

"I think about the pain I've caused, Bobby."

"Don't. Please don't."

"You really believe Miss Porter will be able to see us?"

"Of course."

"It hurts that she will never see Amos."

"We have the pictures, remember?"

Again, he knew she was not listening. They had reached a wide clearing, with grass extending to the river's edge. Suddenly the air was fresher, the smell much reduced, and Lena excitable once more.

"This is where we had picnics! I love the weeping willows along the bank, don't you? Look! A large Coot. See - with the white bill. Look, look - he's running on the water to take off!"

"I see him."

At last, they were on the bridge. It seemed to move with the current, so near were they to water. The cold swirled around them and clung to the railings. Not until they were on the other side did he sense her discomfort.

"What now, Lena?"

"You were crushing me against you."

"Oh. My apologies. Must have heard a bus coming."

Her laughter was instantaneous even if short-lived, for ahead was a dilapidated wooden fence with a gate and a large sign: *Property for Sale, By Appointment Only.* "The end of an era," she said, still quite cheery as they proceeded down the road beyond the fence. "This is the original boundary of the estate. The boarding-school has its own entrance."

"Must be a watchman somewhere."

"We'll say we came to see Miss Porter."

"What else?"

"We could say we were thinking of buying."

"No fear. If necessary we'll storm the ramparts!"

"Okay. But not if we fight doing it."

"Fight?"

"When you get angry we fight, don't we?"

"Good God, Lena. I was only joking."

"I never know what to say to you."

Frustration got the better of him. Stopping as she walked on, he shouted after her: "Lena, one minute you're up, the next you're down. I'm at the end of my tether....Do you understand? Tell me what's bothering you. "

She was irresolute by the side of the road. "Those pictures. They're not very good of Amos."

"All we have, Lena. The old lady will love them. She's expecting us and we must not disappoint her. Do you agree?"

"Yes, Bobby. Thanks." She took a deep breath as if to pull herself together for the task ahead.

The gravel underfoot made walking so ungainly they soon opted for the grass beside the road. At the entrance to the former institution was the faded sign *Waverley Secondary School and Home for Girls*, which ushered them into a driveway covered in falloff from the mature lime trees bordering it on one side.

Across an untended lawn with a neglected pond stood Waverley House. Its monolithic grey-brick structure boasted white sash-widows, a pillared front entrance also in white, and the high, square chimneys they had seen from afar.

"Is this how you remember it?"

"Yes, oh yes." She stepped out of her shoes, picking them up before proceeding. "I used to love this, the fresh grass sprouting through my toes. And look! I can't believe it - the blue double-seat swing is still there. We girls spent many an evening gliding back and forth."

"Not tonight, I'm afraid."

"Why, Bobby?"

"A bit late for romantic nostalgia, don't you think?"

"You won't join me, later?"

"It's broken."

Unsure how to proceed, they decided to go in search of a watchman. In back of the house was the "Caretakers Cottage", where a short, bespectacled man of about sixty, rubbing tired eyes behind horn-rimmed glasses, greeted them at the door.

"Ma lady is havin a wee rest."

"She is expecting us," Lena said.

The little man relented. "It's no' ma afar, Missy. Allow ma tae direct yo' tae the main entrance."

At the paneled front door of the house, they were welcomed by a youthful thirty year old outfitted in starched grey frock and pumps.

"I am Susan. Miss Porter is expecting you, and hopes you will be with us for dinner. A room is ready for you, if you wish to stay over."

They followed Susan into a hall dominated by a mahogany staircase, and blue velvet window coverings. Robert could see excitement in Lena's eyes as she reached back into her childhood.

"At that end of the hallway there is the famous passage leading to her private rooms," she said, breathing in the aroma of waxed floors as she pointed down the hall. "That part of the building was out of bounds to students."

"Miss Porter's study is upstairs, for now," Susan said, as she led the way up the stairs, at the top of which was an alcove housing a porcelain statue of the Virgin.

The study was smaller than Robert had imagined. The old lady was sitting among cushions, in a rocking chair by the front window, which had a balcony overlooking the lawn bordering the drive.

"Your guests to see you, Ma'am," Susan said. "Will you require the refreshments immediately?"

"It's only Leosia and Robert," Lena said, rushing up to the chair to hug her old mentor.

"Tea, in a little while. Thank you, Susan," Miss Porter said, gazing approvingly at Lena as she shed shoulder-bag and coat.

"It's been over five years, and you are lovelier than ever," Miss Porter said with genuine affection.

"This is Robert."

"Of course. Just like the picture on my table. Welcome to our home, Robert," she said, trying unsuccessfully to hide her faltering speech and uncontrollable hands.

"Thank you, Ma'am. You have a beautiful home. I've seen these Georgian houses from afar, but never from the inside."

"For your enjoyment. The house is yours visit, provided you excuse my deplorable condition." With a broad smile, Miss Porter pointed to the chairs by the window. "Bring them closer. Sit, sit.

Dispense with the formalities and tell me your stories."

"You are looking so well," Lena said.

"Just great," Robert said, pretending not to notice tired eyes behind large spectacles that furrowed the cheeks.

"That I can only wish for. You are late, you two," Miss Porter said, looking intently at something beyond the window.

"We tried to...."

"You've missed them. They were bathing, so happily, this afternoon. Such a joy to watch them through my new spyglass," Miss Porter said, reaching down beside her chair and producing a pair of binoculars. "Might be one beneath that Ash-straight ahead."

Lena focused the glasses on the bird-bath. "It's empty now."

"They fly south at this time of year, the Robins do. And the Humming-Birds too, those small creatures that dart about. They fly across oceans. Did you know that? And, do you know what is happening to your old home?" waving her arms in resignation, "they insisted I should retire. How could I refuse them, when most of my girls had left?"

"When we heard the news, we were afraid you might have moved away," Robert said.

"That's their plan. Commercial development. They will tear down the buildings except, I am told, this heritage house. The Lord knows we've had a few of those individuals prowling around lately."

"So sad," Lena said.

Miss Porter shifted in her chair, her words noticeably shaky.

"Maybe it's for the better. This kind of home is a relic of the war. Yet we were hard pressed to place the younger ones when the directive came down."

"After so many years, you deserve a restful life," Lena said.

"Enough of that blarney, child. You know this *is* my life. I thanked God when Waverley girls were like you."

"Don't tell her that, Miss Porter. She is a handful!" Robert said, laughing.

"You're making fun of my favourite daughter, young man."

"Where will you go?" Lena asked.

"Uh. Nowhere, I am sure. Do you think I could get used to another place?"

"Then what will you do?"

"I'll die, my child."

Robert saw the cloud forming over Lena's eyes. "We'll check to see they take good care of you," he said quickly.

Miss Porter understood his concern as she tried to withdraw the remark. "You wouldn't want me to be stuck in a home, would you?"

"No, Ma'am," Lena said.

Equilibrium restored, the old lady was changing the subject.

"Enough of my petty problems. I want to know more about you both – Robert first, then about my little girl here, including all the exotic plans for the future."

The last thing Robert wanted was to talk about himself. He always found it difficult describing his life in Jamaica. For fear listeners would think him boastful, he instinctively reduced everything to the banal.

"Nothing much to tell," he said. "Grew up where the weather is good, then became a runaway. Twice, in fact."

"There must be more to you than that, Robert," Miss Porter said.

"Spoilt rotten, Ma'am. Shipped out to Oxford at twenty to study Classics."

"And?"

"Total fiasco. Returned home. Domestic turmoil. Left again."

"For joining the Air Force?"

"Yes, Ma'am. I prefer not to discuss that."

"I understand. All over, isn't it. You will return home?"

"We're not ready. Not until there's news of Lena's father. In the meantime, I'm accustomed to living and working in London."

"Thank you, Robert. And don't think you are going to get off that easily." Miss Porter said, her affectionate gaze turning to Lena. "Shall I call up the tea, dear Leosia?"

"We are happy just sitting with you."

"Well then, Leosia. I've been in the dark, more or less for the whole time you've been away from Waverly."

"I feel bad about that. I meant to…."

"First: You have told me next to nothing about your terrible loss."

Robert reached out and held Lena's hand. The inevitable question was before her, causing her face to cloud over again.

"I sent you that postcard," Lena said. "We try not to think about Amos."

"Come, come, my child."

"We will never get over Amos, never understand why he was taken from us - after just two months…"

Miss Porter sank back in her chair. "Lena, when you joined us here, you were a lost, lonesome little soul. You rose above misfortune then."

"I try. We both try, in our own way. But, since Amos died I have stopped…."

"Not like you, my child. I am not scolding you, now. Believe me, I understand. Trying is the only way. You know that better than most. The ability to crawl through life's debris and come out on the bright side is one of your strengths."

"We struggle to forget. Instead we remember with greater and greater clarity," Lena said.

Robert was certain that she would crack. She had not spoken of Amos with such candour for many months, and already there were signs of stress in the way she gripped the sides of her chair.

Miss Porter must have seen it too because she added: "You must remember Amos in each other."

"Yes. That's how it should be," Robert said. "And remember each other too." But he knew there was something bothering the old lady when she reached into the folds of her dress and found a handkerchief.

"I can preach, because I too lost a child. Ages ago," she said.

The shock for Lena was immediate. "Never heard that! You told us you lost your husband in the Great War, that's all."

"My turn to own up, then. He was no husband. I never saw the rascal after the first three months of my pregnancy. Don't know what ever happened to him."

"I am mortified. You never let on."

"No. A convenient story mine was too. I waited for him for years, but never looked for him."

"Why not, Miss Porter?" Lena asked.

The old lady hesitated before she replied, as if she was not sure what words were appropriate. "Don't we women hold very close to our hearts the memory of things we have mislaid, for fear of losing them forever?"

"Yes, you're right..."

"That way, lost things are not really lost - provided we remember where they might be, and do nothing about looking."

Robert knew exactly what she meant. It had been the story of their lives. "On the bright side, there is a faint hope of her father's return."

Miss Porter beamed. "Swell! Have you heard from him?"

"No. But he may be in Siberia," Lena said. "The Russians are slow to release information, much less the prisoners themselves.

The British authorities assure me they are following up a lead...."

"Wonderful news," the old lady said, settling back in her chair with a serine look on her face. "So. Tell us. What has befallen you since you upped and left us?"

"You mean from 1943? I've told you...."

"Yes. I get mixed up sometimes.... Emphasis on the juicy bits, please - at least until Susan brings the tea."

Lena looked trapped. Without warning, she was in a confessional with no way out.

"Some things are harder than others," she said, avoiding the old lady's expectant gaze.

"Nothing to fear in your old home, dearest," Miss Porter smiled reassuringly. "The ordinary bits then."

Lena hesitated, like a diver about to jump off the high-board.

"You must know that I went up to London."

"Of course. To take up nursing."

"I was just eighteen in '43, as you may remember. I explored the city for a month before joining St. Barts that October. My English was very good, I did well academically and made lots of friends. I found it exhilarating being part of that great hospital. On weekends during the summer months, when the evenings were still light, we girls went into the West End for the dances, especially the week-end affairs at the Empress Ballroom. There a brass band played most Saturday nights. Sometimes we went to one or other of the big hotels. I usually wore the dark blue dress you gave me. Very fetching, with the thin straps. You remember it?"

"Yes I do, Leosia." Miss Porter was beaming with pleasure as Lena waxed strong.

"We girls never had escorts. We just lined up at the edge of the dance-floor, waiting for the young men to pluck up courage. When there were only a few of them around, we danced with each other. Such fun! Sometimes, we were courted by older men on leave from their units abroad. There was a balcony upstairs the Empress, for those of drinking age. It had tables and, from those closest to the parapet overlooking the dance floor, drinkers could view the girls below. We never went upstairs, mind you. They would be ogling us from afar, until one of us struck their fancy and the chase began. I was usually dead by the end of an evening."

"I remember evenings like that," Miss Porter said, getting into the story. "During the twenties there even were midday dances."

"We love dancing," Robert said, relieved to see Lena in good spirits, maybe too good, because she was soon into things of which he knew nothing. Did he want to know?

"In April '45 there was an urgent call from the Front for volunteers. Trainee medics of all stripes were asked to help for short periods in a camp in northwestern Germany, liberated by the British-Canadian army. Apart from being fluent in Polish, I was also quite comfortable in German, and, especially after I heard that many of the inmates were Polish, I pleaded to serve beside a close friend. Miriam, an RN from Liverpool and ten years my senior, was my supervisor at the time. Neither of us knew what we would be facing, but I was excited because, at last, there was a chance I might learn something of father's whereabouts. You may have read about this camp - near the village of Belsen."

Robert began to feel uncomfortable. The confessional tone of Lena's reminiscences was disturbing in itself. Where was she going with these revelations? "You've kept me in the dark about this, Lena."

She would not be distracted. "Being spring, of course the countryside was green and very beautiful. The tulips were in bloom, and among the trees there were carpets of bluebells. Yet the horrors....I can't find words to describe them to you, although the camp is as vivid in my mind today as the day I went through those gates for the first time."

"I saw something of it in the newspapers," Miss Porter said.

"The wooden barracks - the smell," Lena continued, as if in a trance. "The sickly odor of bodies that were stacked up along fences, inside walls, on the cots where the unfortunates had died: bluish heaps decomposing amidst excrement that was ankle deep almost everywhere. And the living-dead: too weak to get up off bunks that were covered in the stuff."

The most upsetting thing for Robert was the fact that for nearly two years Lena had kept all these things to herself.

"How awful, Lena," Miss Porter said.

"After a week of futile efforts to help them, hundreds were still dying every day in our section of the camp. I was working under Miriam. She put on a good face, but was coping with the situation no better than I was. It is impossible to describe the helplessness we felt dealing with the living dead, the outstretched hands, the eyes in deep holes, the painful whispers. Every day teams of us helped to carry the bodies out and throw them into mass graves dug by bulldozers. After a while we could not keep up with the numbers."

"Terrible, just terrible," Miss Porter said.

"You had to keep at it, day and night, somehow, or go mad," Lena continued, ruminating, rather than responding to the old lady's incredulity. "Hardly anyone spoke, as if noise of any kind would disturb the dead. All we wanted was for the nightmare to end. And yet, with all the suffering and death all around us, our greatest concern was for the children." There was the new edge to Lena's story, an urgency bordering on desperation.

"We became attached to a Polish girl of about six years old. When we discovered her she was lying beside the body of her mother, who had died sometime before. A skeleton with pallid flesh drawn over bone and a few strands of black hair on her head, the child was in the later stages of starvation but could not take food. We moved her, cleaned her and for a day watched her die, accompanied by countless others.... Unbearable...."

"Lena, stop it!" Robert said, to no avail.

"The last time we saw her she was one of the bodies being

shoveled by a bulldozer across the compound, to the open grave...."

"This is all news to me," he said, helpless before the onslaught of words and images.

"Forgive me, Robert. Please forgive me," she said, reaching out and grabbing his arm without a response. "This was supposed to remain between Miriam and me."

"Don't tell me! That's why ...."

"Keeps getting worse," Miss Porter said.

Robert was holding fingers to his ears to emphasize disapproval. "I cannot listen to any more of this. Call me when you are through." Rising, he bowed to the old lady and, without looking at Lena, collected his coat. "Please excuse me, Ma'am. I must take a walk."

"Don't leave, Robert, darling. You should hear this, painful as it is."

"I've heard enough, Lena. We agreed we would not speak of the war. Forget?"

"Forgive me, please. I must finish what I started. Miss Porter is willing to listen, even if you are not."

Already in the middle of the room, he hesitated, passing his coat from one hand to the other, before deciding.

"Later, maybe. No offence, Miss Porter. I'll be downstairs, or wondering about," he said as he closed the door behind him.

The story thus far is one the particulars of which I am confident are factual. However, after Robert's withdrawal from the meeting at Waverley in October 1948, what transpired between Lena and Miss Porter is less certain, especially if I were to take seriously various denials of later years. However, those I regard as entirely self-serving to the claimant I have not allowed to cast doubt on the course of events documented below. This I believe is as close a version of the truth as is possible to aver in the circumstances.

Lena and Miss Porter sat waiting for Robert to return. Surely, he would have a change of heart about his sudden departure.

"Lena, dear, seems I have come between you both." The old woman looked defeated. Her sadness was real.

"Not your fault, Miss Porter. Never that. I promised Robert I wouldn't bring up the war. Little does he know there are many other things I couldn't speak to you about - in his company. I'm relieved he's gone, really I am."

"What sort of things, child?"

"Bad things. I've had no one to confide in for eighteen months, and they are a burden I cannot carry alone."

"So glad to have you back home. Tell this old lady what is troubling you."

"Again, I don't know where to begin. I am so ashamed. I have paid for it something dreadful. And yet I had - so to say - few reservations at the time. I regarded the war and what it had brought me, as ample excuses for my recklessness. I look back and all I see are terrible things that justified my rebellion. After I came here, my mother was killed... I became a refugee. Soon after, the realization I might never see father again. Then, later on...."

"There, there. You'll see him again," Miss Porter said. "Right now, I'm concerned about your health."

"If you wish, Miss Porter, call it *mental* health. It's why Robert went out just now. He does not understand it, and cannot face up to his own disabilities. Neither of us can live with guilt."

"I understand that war changes people. But guilt is for the politicians and generals to bear."

"Thank you, Miss Porter. I love you for saying that. And yet, I can only pray God will forgive me for the bad things I have done. God knows I have been punished for them. It began some months before Belsen. Miriam and I had become very close, although I could not say that just now. Robert knows nothing about our love affair. I was very young and impressionable, and comforted – flattered really - by her avowed affection for me. Strong willed and experienced, she had been places and done things I never dreamed of. She was beautiful and strong, with no inhibitions, and her wild streak was too infectious to resist. Not that I am excusing what we did. I felt deeply for her. At first I asked the Blessed Virgin to understand; then, after a while, I begged for forgiveness. Every day I prayed not to love Miriam, or she me."

"You need say no more."

"Forgive me, I must. In the autumn of '44 we rented a flat together. We were very happy - enjoyed going to the Empress together. Can you believe that, Miss Porter?"

"Yes, even if I can't approve of your beastly carrying on."

"It grieves me to upset you like this. Never spoken of these things - not to Robert, hardly to myself, except in the night when I cannot sleep."

"It's okay, Lena. I don't have to understand. You know you can tell me whatever troubles you. After all, I've not lived a completely sheltered life, you know."

"I want Robert to know - he should know. I just can't tell him yet."

"No, Lena. Don't tell me your sins now, just to be able to tell Robert later. They may destroy you both."

"Miriam and I were a great comfort to each other. We lived in fear of the V2 rockets over London. I could tell him that."

"Frightening. Yet, not for the telling."

"Miriam's greatest fear was scandal, so we ended up renting separate apartments. This she preferred, if only because she was not without male suitors whom she played, one against the other. We must be very careful to fool the crowd: so she said. Guilt had nothing to do with it. Only image. I don't believe she ever had a bad conscience about our lifestyle, as I did."

"Your friend is not made like you, dearest."

"On occasion, she went off on overseas jobs for the hospital. In the following March, she went to Rome, where she met a young man, a Canadian on an assignment for the government. They may have had a brief encounter, I don't know. Then later, as I told you, we found ourselves shattered by Bergen Belsen, for which I had volunteered purely for selfish reasons to do with my father."

"Not to be ashamed of, Leosia. Doing God's work, you were."

"After we returned from Germany, Miriam began to act strangely. It came to a head after her Canadian friend invited her to a rowing party in Richmond, where she got off with Robert. My Robert!"

"You mean you were complicit in that?"

"No, of course not, Miss Porter. I didn't know her Canadian friend, and certainly not Robert at that time. Needless to say, I wasn't invited to the party - following which, without much warning, Miriam broke it off with me."

Miss Porter cupped her face in her hands. "So, your female lover plays around, and finally takes off with your future partner. Diabolical."

"Quite ruthless, I'll admit. But in a good cause, so she thought. Seven years older than Robert, she knew how to get to him. And yet she also loved him in her ambiguous way."

"More exciting, maybe."

"Two natures, yes. She moved into his flat with hardly a word to me about the matter. That was early in May. Given of our new living arrangements, I found it convenient to assume this was just another case of wanderlust. On the contrary, it persisted beyond that, and the longer it went on the more hurt I became. I actually gave up on ever seeing her again, especially after she resigned from the hospital later that month."

"Obviously, that was not the end."

"No. She turned up at my graduation. Then out of nowhere, six months later, I received a letter of apology telling me she had been superstitious about moving in with Robert, and begging forgiveness. I felt I was being manipulated, but confused and alone I agreed to meet her."

Just then, there was a sound in the passage of metal on wood, and Susan appeared in the doorway.

"The tea is here, Ma'am."

"Did you look after the gentleman?"

"He had his tea served in the library."

"We will have ours now, please."

Susan wheeled in the trolley and positioned it beside Miss Porter's chair, then stood by as if unsure of what to say.

"In accordance with the gentleman's wishes, Ma'am, I made up two rooms for the guests," she said, and quickly excused herself.

They were alone again, and Miss Porter was confused.

"Did I hear her say that you sleep in separate rooms?"

"Yes, Miss Porter."

"Not good, child. Not good."

Lena pretended not to hear the reprimand. One life of sin was enough for one evening. The irony was Miss Porter would approve of separate rooms if she knew the truth.

"He is going to leave me. Soon, I believe."

"Why ever would you say that?"

"He's had enough of my inabilities, since Amos …."

"Thank God he hasn't left already! It's up to you now. There's no problem that a young couple can't overcome, except one…."

"No. He's not seeing…. At least, I don't think so."

"Good. You can wipe away those tears, young lady. Maybe have some tea now, and continue our discussion afterwards?"

The problem for Lena was the "afterwards" part. As she poured the tea, she felt certain that what she had to say further would make no sense to someone as far removed from her world as Miss Porter was.

"You were telling me about the time your friend suddenly reappears."

"Yes. We met at a coffee-shop on the Strand - a cold winter's day, yet she turned up in leather jacket and heels. Instead of being down in the dumps, as her letter had suggested, she was the usual flamboyant, outspoken Miriam, embellished with a touch of bravado as she laid bare the plan she had devised for us."

"And?"

"It had to do with the child we lost at Belsen."

Miss Porter put her cup down to gesticulate disapprovingly. "I knew something like that was afoot."

"Robert had been easy prey for her, she said. Although she was genuinely fond of him in her way, it had not worked...."

"I dare not ask..."

"Her crazy plan had been to get pregnant, then break off the affair before he learned about it. No one would be hurt, see? Just another fling, with a catch, of course. She was so wild. Still is, I believe."

"Karamba!"

"Robert did not know it. She had had a miscarriage, and gave up on her chances...."

"Go on." Miss Porter was visibly shaken, but wanting to know more.

"She had a good reason for trying. I was partly to blame. You see, during those frightful days in Germany we had made a solemn promise to each other to adopt a child, in memory of the many we saw die so horribly. For myself, maybe a romantic notion, maybe to fill a void, nothing more. But not for Miriam. So much so, she took it one step further, all on her own."

"Why then did she not tell you about it, and save you the unhappiness?"

"Because silence allowed her to live in denial. She was convinced her plan would be jinxed, doomed to failure, if she spelled it out for me. She might lose me as a partner, something she thought a *fait accompli* would avoid."

"Her plan failed anyway."

"Yes."

Miss Porter straightened and rearranged the chair cushions for the umpteenth time, before saying what obviously was bothering her.

"If I'm following you, Miriam was desperate. She went off without telling you why. Now, she waltzes back – let me guess: to ask you to do evil for her. Is that it?"

"Yes, except not evil in her mind."

"That you should prostitute yourself before her erstwhile lover?"

"Oh, it would be very easy, she soon assured me. That measure of reason, then the laugh that admitted the absurdity of it all , those eyes I had forgotten were blue until I was caught in their gaze. Suddenly there was no alternative. I had put myself in a position where I felt I had to accept this outlandish proposal."

"You expect me to believe that? What about Robert?"

"She convinced me that he was tired of her; that he was the kind of man that needed a woman. I really would warm to him, and he to me. When the brief affair was over, we would be together again. By the time the child was born, Robert would be far away."

Miss Porter was silent, pulling back as if to study her from afar. "Seems you stretched yourself to do this abominable deed." Anger, disbelief, reprimand, were prominent in the old lady's heightened agitation, a rejection punctuated by her hands disappearing from view.

"I did not mean it that way, Miss Porter. I don't know what I intended. I agreed to meet him. That was all I promised. Of course I was not to tell him anything about Germany, or about the two of us, of course. What Miriam did not realize was that I had lost interest in our affair. A convenient way to put off telling her was to go with Robert - if it came to that, as she had asked."

"Actions speak louder than convenient outs, Lena," Miss Porter said, now pointedly less endearing.

"I went to see him at their apartment. They were still together then, but Miriam arranged that I should pick her up there, when she would have left for the cinema already. "

"And?"

"I don't know what came over me. I was twenty-one and had been through a lot. I did not understand my attraction to Robert. However, I knew immediately on meeting him that I could never step back to my former life."

The tension slowly left the old lady's face.

"I think I understand," she said, apparently relieved.

"Robert felt badly about leaving Miriam, as he understood the break-up, although she'd given him reason to believe she wanted it. As an afterthought I had no qualms about being with him."

"Falling in love is easy, my child. The difficult part is what love becomes of it, over time."

"Yes. We know that now. I was afraid of the feelings I had for Robert. I knew he was the person I wanted, but I could not help feeling I was betraying Miriam. I hesitated about marriage."

"Then what?"

"I got pregnant. Sealed my fate. How could I tell you when I had not said anything to you about marriage? Or tell Miriam, when I had no intention of going back to her?"

"Made you feel more, not less guilty for that."

"Yes. The original intention was wrong - even if I changed my mind afterwards. That is how it seemed to me. I had tempted God, in more ways than one. Sinned, again and again. I knew He would punish me."

"Don't say that, Leosia."

"It's true, Miss Porter. God did punish me, horribly. Little

Amos was a beautiful child, but the labour had been torture, too hard. In the end, they had to use high forceps. He was badly damaged. Then infection turned up in both of us. There was nothing anyone could do. He lingered for two months, then died…before I had the courage to write you. My life was at an end."

"I had no idea," Miss Porter said, rising to take Lena in her arms.

"The more I realized the bad things I had done, the more I despaired, the more Amos's death weighed on me, I withdrew from the idea of marriage, from Robert. Can't respond to him, as I could before Amos died. He's leaving me. Right now, he's trying to find the words…."

"I believe the medical term for it is Melancholia. Seems to me you are *both* suffering from a chronic state of mourning. It's called remorse, not forgiving yourself. If guilt damages the heart, remorse kills the soul. Surely, the answer is to have another child."

"The doctors say I can't. I've try to explain that to Robert, who will not hear of an adoption. So I've failed all around. He's got demons of his own. Miriam was right when she said he was a needy person. Ironically, she filled a void I can't."

"At least her conscience was clear about it all."

"Yes."

"Yours is not, and you've made Robert suffer for your sins."

"Yes. Please forgive my laying all this on you," Lena said.

The double-seat swing was immovable. Robert sat on the floorboard between the seats, looking at the night sky and a leaf-strewn lawn. From the pond ahead he could hear the rriiibiit rriiibiit of a lonely frog. Did she not say she would be here? Why was she not? Could he expect otherwise when he had dismissed her suggestion to meet as pointless nostalgia?

So, the least she could have done was to come looking for him. Was this not one of those loyalty tests she usually failed? The silly games that he played against her without her knowing. And yet, they confirmed what he already knew. He had walked out on Miriam, much as Lena had withdrawn from him. Why could he not accept it and move on?

Lena, Lena, beautiful Lena. That first evening she had seemed so innocent, so unblemished by the world he had known. All he had to do was spirit her away in the blush of womanhood and give her all she had ever wanted. Sentiment makes such fools of us, he thought. But she was not the wispy, innocent girl he had imagined - rather a woman who had seen the horrors of death and dying, up close. Why had she not spoken of those things before today?

The moonlit evening had the chill running through it, just as she had predicted. The stars were brighter now, phosphorescent asterisks on a dark canvas. He would always remember her eyes, bright and expressive of inner fire - the light that went out with Amos.

We used to love the nightlife, Bobby - dancehalls and all.

You don't want to go out anymore.

I used to, remember?

Not very well.

Couldn't we go away then?

That wouldn't solve anything, Lena.

I know how you feel, but don't hurt me.

I try not to do that, and you don't know how I feel. The dance-floor's empty. We count the steps to no effect, because there's no music. You really believe that, Bobby?

Yes. What else am I to believe?

Tell me you will stay, even if I can't help myself.

Stop! Soon we'll be all reconciled and making stupid promises.

We're just talking, aren't we?

Nowadays we just argue, Lena.

Okay. Let's not, for a change. Speak to me, Bobby. Tell me what bothers you about the war.

Forget it. What about you? There's a saying back home: "Some things not good to talk."

What things, Bobby? I just wish we could have a serious discussion once in a while.

Serious discussion begins in the bedroom, Lena. You gave up on that some time ago.

Miriam told me you were awarded a medal for bravery or something. Is that true?

I refused it.

Why, Bobby. Tell me why or I'll sit on your face.

For surviving. In any case the war is over, so fuck it.

It's not, Bobby. You don't sleep at night.

Neither do you. I could ask you the same question.

Don't start that, Bobby. We're just talking, remember?

About nothing.

So, tell me what you refused a medal for.

For torching people, God damn it.

What people?

Innocents, all of them.

How do you mean? What are you saying?

Don't be naïve, Lena. What do you think the bombs were for? But you were doing a job!

Yes. Like the job against Hamburg in '43. We flew past the target on our initial approach, without releasing any ordinance. Everyone on the ground believed the Halifaxes were en route to another city, or maybe the Russian front. Then we turned around, and came back over unprepared, densely populated Hamburg - dropping phosphorous and other stuff….

But, darling….

Fire bombs – raging fire-storms enveloping everyone and everything in their paths. Any idea what that means?

That's horrid.

Could smell the burning bodies, and pictured the human torches jumping into the canal - reigniting if they got out of the water.

Holy Mary, Bobby.

Tens of thousands died, mostly women and children, even those in safety-bunkers.

How?

Asphyxiation.

What do you mean?

Fire storms suck the air out. Mothers died joined at the mouth to their dead infants.

Surely, such things were done only by the enemy.

You're looking at him, Lena. In the bomb-bay I pulled the trigger.

Don't say more, Bobby.

I knew you wouldn't understand.

I do and I don't, Bobby. I love you and am glad you told me.

Come here, Lena.

The times she had responded to him, and the times she had not. Instinctively he tried to activate the swing, but it refused to move. He went into the house, where his bedroom was in the basement. Apart from a single bed it contained an oak dresser, a stand-alone cupboard, and a washstand replete with a baroque porcelain basin and goblet. After shaving, he threw on the clean shirt Lena brought and proceeded up the central staircase to the dining room.

When he got there, the meal was already laid on - lamb and mint sauce with wild rice and vegetables. Sitting together on one side of the table, the three women were telling stories and toasting one another. Miss Porter and Susan were in good form, raising their glasses to him when he arrived. He joined in, hardly seeing them.

For there she was, wearing the black cocktail dress he had given her when Amos was born, a dress she had never worn before tonight. In a way he was glad he was sitting on the opposite side of the table, for from this vantage point he could be charmed by the golden glint hiding among golden swirls, and seduced by at the cut of pale shoulders. Was she really as happy as she seemed to be at this moment? What had she told the old lady about him? What was there to tell, anyway?

Soon after they finished dessert Miss Porter began to wilt. She refused coffee, and only sipped the liqueur, before motioning to Susan to help her stand for the last toast. There followed tearful goodnights before she was wheeled off to her room.

Alone with Lena, Robert was aware of a strange elation in the air, quite the opposite of his forebodings earlier that evening. Moved by an overwhelming need to hold her he said, "You look stunning tonight. You didn't tell me you were packing such good clothes."

Her smile was almost mischievous. "Borrowed shoes, and all. Only for you."

"For me?"

"Yes. Just a thought."

"I'm honoured. I even forgive you for not joining me in that broken-down swing."

"I had no idea, after what you said. Miss Porter and I spent the time talking. You know…."

"Telling tales on me?"

She sighed. "Not one. I had a lovely afternoon, even if it was difficult, in part. So you see, I must go to bed before I fall over."

She rose from the table and stretched, so that she stood very erect with her head back and eyes closed. The moment was not lost on him.

"Is your room comfortable?" He asked, hoping to delay her departure.

"Yes, of course - thanks for arranging it." She patted his arm, before walking purposefully to the door.

Not a little confused by her demeanour, and annoyed with himself for not protesting her departure more ardently, he remained behind to finish his coffee. Had he not made tentative plans that did not include her? If so why did seeing her this evening bring back such visceral longings? He must steel himself to put such feelings aside, he thought. There was no going back to what had befallen them this past year. If he overcame the urge to revisit that, it may even assuage the misery of their tragic loss.

Today's revelations put Lena in a whole new light. In fact, he met a different woman from the one with whom he had been living. Suddenly she was strong and purposeful, even when she continued to be the vulnerable person he knew, one who could look after herself. Was this not the catalyst he needed to do what he had to do?

Ultimately, that would require his leaving this godforsaken part of the world. He had done his duty to king and country. What was left for him here if he stayed, but more years of January? With one proviso, maybe, the small space that would remain in the recesses of his mind: the one occupied by Miriam. She was the woman who sought him out, who showed him what it meant to live without inhibitions, and yet, she was the commitment he walked away from without compunction. Was his current suffering punishment for that?

At 9:30, with the house closing down, he took off to his room.

For some time he had conjuring up the idea of a home-coming. What would it be like to be completely reconciled with his father, visit his mother wherever she might be? Would he be able to involve himself in a business for which he cared little? To these questions he had no answers, except that he was twenty seven years of age and the time had come for him to look to the future.

Of course, putting any plan together without involving Lena was difficult, if not impossible. But it also was impossible, if not immoral, to continue deceiving her. Hence, the necessity to level with her as soon as possible. Once he had put the past behind him for good and he was back in the sun, the enigma that was Lena would lose its emotive power.

Very tired, he was determined to fall asleep with his vision of tomorrow prominent among the sheep. And yet sleep eluded him. Instead, feelings of uncertainty morphed into dozes that left him more tired than before; until, in a dream, he saw Lena standing by the door, her bold nakedness luminous and defying the moonlight. Except that he was awake, and she was terrifyingly real. With arms outstretched she came to him and her coolness covered his craving soul.

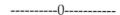

During 1949 I visited Robert and Lena twice, and had occasion to speak candidly, and at some length, with Lena before her baby was born. Afterwards, she was very happy to see Miriam, who surprised her by turning up at the hospital. But of her father she waited for news that never came.

She was gone before Robert received word that Miss Porter was ailing and calling for her. At first, he was of two minds about visiting the old lady because he wished to keep the news from her. He soon thought better of it. After all, he owed it to Lena that Adelaide Porter see the baby, who was then two months old.

With great affection for the Miss Porter, Robert told me of his taking the baby to see her in a nursing home. Jaundiced and, as he described her, a bamboo-like skeleton with skin drawn tight on face and limbs, she cuddled the infant by her side and wept as Robert told her of Lena's last days.

He found it curious that Miss Porter should take such an interest in the news about Miriam's surprise visits to Lena's bedside, but also that Lena had been so moved in receiving her.

He felt certain the old lady was sending him a message when she summoned up the strength to pull him closer to her and whisper in his ear about how fondly Lena had spoken of Miriam the year before; about great friendships and how they survive even death. To my knowledge, this was all Robert ever gleaned of the conversation between Lena and Adelaide Porter after he left the room on that afternoon in 1948.

In that year of promise, 1950, Robert and Miriam picked up where they had left off, living together once again in Richmond on Thames. There, two years later, they married and continued to make the best of their stormy union for another four years before news came that old man Stroud had died. The time had come for Robert to heed his wife's promptings and take his family home.

AFTERWORD

The stories in this book are fictional in nature and content. Any resemblance that the characters portrayed may have to actual persons, living or dead; or the incidents depicted to actual events, past or present, is coincidental and not intended.

Because of Jamaica's size and familiar topography, some readers may try to identify named locales with actual estates, villages, or areas of the country. However, there is no intention on the author's part to actualize places beyond the requirements of the stories. Likewise, in the interests of anonymity, various liberties have been taken with regard to posited locales outside of the island.

ABOUT THE AUTHOR

Dereck C. Sale was born in 1941 and grew up in Jamaica. As a youth, he spent nine years in the Jesuit academies of Campion and St. Georges College, before he moved to England to pursue his professional studies. He became the youngest partner in an international firm of Chartered Accountants on his return to the island, where he and his Swedish wife remained for twelve years, and where their four children were born. Today the extended family live in Canada. Over the decades, Sale's writings on professional, economic, and political issues have been published in newspapers and financial journals in several countries. His first book *Testament of the Third Man,* appeared in 2007.

Cover drawing by Fred Sale

Cover enhancement and formatting by Crystal MacDonald, of *Concept Design*